THE SWAMI'S RING

NANCY DREW MYSTERY STORIES®

THE SWAMI'S RING

by
Carolyn Keene

Illustrated by
Paul Frame

WANDERER BOOKS

Published by Simon & Schuster, New York

Copyright © 1981 by Stratemeyer Syndicate
All rights reserved
including the right of reproduction
in whole or in part in any form
Published by WANDERER BOOKS
A Simon & Schuster Division of
Gulf & Western Corporation
Simon & Schuster Building
1230 Avenue of the Americas
New York, New York 10020

Manufactured in the United States of America
10 9 8 7 6 5 4 3 2 1

NANCY DREW and NANCY DREW MYSTERY STORIES
are trademarks of Stratemeyer Syndicate,
registered in the United States Patent
and Trademark Office

WANDERER and colophon are trademarks of Simon & Schuster

Library of Congress Cataloging in Publication Data

Keene, Carolyn.
The swami's ring.

(Nancy Drew mystery stories; 61)
Summary: When an amnesia victim appears in
River Heights with a royal Hindu ring in his
possession, Nancy Drew is called in to help learn
his identity.
[1. Mystery and detective stories. 2. Amnesia—
Fiction] I. Frame, Paul, ill. II. Title.
III. Series: Keene, Carolyn. Nancy Drew mystery
stories; 61)
PZ7.K23   Nan no. 61 [Fic]   81-11580
ISBN 0-671-42344-4   AACR2
ISBN 0-671-42345-2 (pbk.)

Contents

1

Mysterious Patient

"Nancy, would you come over to Rosemont Hospital and help solve a mystery?"

Mystery! That was all the girl detective needed to hear from her former schoolmate, Lisa Scotti, who was now a nurse.

"Sounds exciting," Nancy said eagerly. "Tell me about it."

"A young man was just brought into emergency with bad bruises. He has amnesia— can't remember who he is, where he has been, where he was going, or what happened."

"Who found him?" Nancy asked.

"Some people from out of state. They had stopped along a wooded highway near the airport to stretch their legs and discovered him at the bottom of a cliff. Apparently, he fell or was pushed off. I'm surprised he doesn't have any broken bones."

"Me too," Nancy said, adding quickly, "I'll be right over. 'Bye—"

"Wait—don't hang up," Lisa interrupted. "Visiting hours don't begin until eleven."

Nancy glanced at her wristwatch. It was only ten o'clock.

"In that case, why don't I offer to do some volunteer work at Rosemont? Then I'll be able to see Cliff almost anytime."

Lisa giggled. "How did you know that's what all us nurses call him?"

"I didn't." Nancy laughed.

"Meet you on the fifth floor. Cliff's in Room 502."

As soon as Lisa clicked off, Nancy dialed the hospital phone number. Since she had attended an orientation program for Rosemont volunteers the previous summer, she was no stranger to the hospital. Surely she could start right away. At least, she hoped so.

"Nancy dear," Hannah called out when the girl dropped the receiver into its cradle, "would you rather have fish or fowl for dinner?"

"I'll take either so long as it's garnished with savory clues!" Nancy teased.

"Now be serious," Mrs. Gruen replied, poking her head out of the kitchen.

Over the years, a warm and wonderful cameraderie had grown between the young woman and the Drews' housekeeper. She had helped rear Nancy since the girl was three, when Mrs. Drew had passed away.

"I am being serious." Nancy smiled. Her blue eyes almost danced as sunlight captured her pretty face and reddish-blond hair.

"Don't tell me you're off on a mystery of your own before you finish the case you and your dad are working on," Hannah replied saucily. She was hoping the answer would be no. "What will your father say?"

Carson Drew was a prominent attorney in River Heights who had recently become embroiled in problems of the town's summer music festival. The evening before, he had told Nancy his fear that it might be forced to close because of a squabble among some performers. As he frequently did, Mr. Drew asked his gifted eighteen-year-old daughter for advice.

"If you mean that Dad's going to worry

whether I'll have time to work on two mysteries at the same time—" Nancy started to say.

"That's precisely what I mean."

Nancy did not agree, however. She knew how Hannah worried about her, but could not help teasing her once in a while.

"When Dad comes home, tell him I'm in the hospital."

"What?" the woman gulped.

"Not as a patient, though."

The housekeeper shook her head while Nancy pecked her cheek and said good-bye. Driving across town, she noticed the billboard announcement for the River Heights Music Festival, but kept her thoughts concentrated on Rosemont Hospital, where she shortly found herself.

After parking the car, she hurried into the building to register as a volunteer, then went directly to an elevator and pressed the button. The door slid open a moment later, but as she stepped forward, a large, burly man with a heavy, black beard shoved her aside.

"Hey—" she cried as the stranger hurried ahead and pushed an inside button, but the door closed before Nancy could enter. She glanced up at the bank of lights overhead. "He's stopping at the fifth floor!" she murmured. "I hope I don't bump into him again!"

It seemed to take forever for the elevator to return, but at last the young detective was on her way upstairs. Lisa was waiting for her.

"Some creep got off the elevator a minute ago," the nurse said, "and practically knocked me down."

"That makes two of us," Nancy replied as they walked toward Room 502.

When they were within a few feet of Cliff's room, they heard short, quick gasps and ran inside.

"Oh, no! Stop!" Lisa shrieked when she saw the hands of the bearded stranger clutching at Cliff's neck.

"Get away from him!" Nancy demanded. She and Lisa grabbed the man's arms.

Angrily, he wrenched himself away from the girls. "Where's the ring you stole?" he growled at Cliff.

"I'm going to call the police if you don't—" Lisa threatened.

Now the man stiffened. He loosened his fingers from Cliff's neck, allowing the patient to

11

slip back against the pillow. Cliff moaned softly and opened his eyes halfway, only to shut them again.

"Who are you?" Nancy asked the intruder.

He whirled on his heels and stormed out into the corridor.

"Come back here!" Nancy insisted. She hurried after him as fast as she could, but his long legs carried him swiftly away from her into the elevator which now descended.

Instantly, Nancy dashed through the stairwell door. She raced down the steps, taking two at a time, and upon reaching the main floor, burst across the lobby to the entrance.

"Oh!" she muttered in disappointment. The stranger had disappeared into a waiting tan-colored car with a blue racing stripe on the trunk. The vehicle sped down the street.

Puffs of exhaust from the tail pipe succeeded in covering up the license plate so that Nancy could not decipher it. Disgusted, she returned to Cliff's room, where Lisa was giving him a small cup of water.

"This is my friend, Nancy Drew," the young nurse said, introducing the two.

The patient, a rugged-faced man with light

13

brown hair, nodded weakly. "I wish I could tell you my name," he said with a hint of laughter in his voice.

"Cliff will do for the time being," Nancy replied. "You had a pretty rough experience just a few minutes ago. Do you know who that man was?"

"No, not at all."

"Nancy is an amateur detective," Lisa quickly inserted, "and she wants to help you."

Cliff smiled again. "Tell me about some of your cases."

The girl detective blushed modestly.

"As a matter of fact," Lisa put in, "Nancy has been out of the country for her two most recent mysteries. She found *The Secret in the Old Lace* in Belgium and went to Greece to decipher *The Greek Symbol Mystery*."

"You have an excellent memory," Nancy remarked, suddenly realizing what she had said. "Oh, I'm sorry, Cliff."

"This old head's not that sensitive." The patient chuckled. "I'm sure my memory was at least as good as yours, Nancy—once upon a time."

Before she could say more, he closed his eyes

14

sleepily and Lisa beckoned Nancy out into the corridor.

"I'd like to tell Bess and George about all of this," Nancy said.

Bess Marvin and George Fayne were cousins and Nancy's closest friends who often helped her solve mysteries.

"The more brains we get thinking about Cliff's identity," Lisa answered, "the quicker we'll find out who he is."

"Exactly."

Nancy excused herself to telephone the Marvin home. To her delight, Bess answered.

"Just a minute, Nancy. Let me put George on, too. She's here."

"Great, because I need to talk to *both* of you."

"Uh-oh," Bess said. "I have a feeling we're in for another adventure—n-nothing dangerous, I hope."

Nancy laughed lightly while her friend called George to an extension phone. Then, as briefly as possible, the girl told them about Cliff.

"I'd like you to meet him," Nancy said. "Can you come over to the hospital?"

"Sure," Bess and George chorused eagerly.

By the time they reached Rosemont Hospital, Cliff was awake again, and Nancy introduced her friends. Afterwards, George asked if any identification had been found on the patient.

"Apparently not," Nancy said.

"The only thing he was carrying was a knapsack," Lisa advised.

She pulled the heavy canvas bag out of the closet.

"Cliff, would you object if I went through it?" Nancy asked.

"No, of course not."

While everyone watched, she removed several articles of clothing and an envelope with money in it. Then her fingers felt the lining of the bag. An unexpected thickness in the material suggested a hidden pocket.

"Did you find something else?" Bess asked, breaking the silence.

"Could be."

She opened the pocket and rolled the contents into her palm.

"Don't keep us in suspense," George begged as Nancy took her hand out.

When she opened it, everyone gasped at the girl's discovery. It was a large, gold ring, extremely ornate and obviously meant for a very fat finger!

"That would swim on Cliff's hand," Lisa observed.

Nancy glanced at the young man, whose eyes were riveted on the unusual ring. Was this the one he had been accused of stealing?

2

Tommy's Accident

"Cliff," Nancy said, holding the ring out to him, "does this mean anything to you?"

He blinked his eyes as if struggling to remember. "I—I, no, it doesn't."

"I don't think it should be left unguarded in this closet," Nancy announced. "Can we put it in the hospital safe until I come back with my magnifying glass? I'd like to examine it further."

"Definitely," Lisa replied, "if that's all right with Cliff."

Lisa promised to take the ring downstairs as soon as she gave him his medication. Nancy, meanwhile, led Bess and George to the office of

Dr. Randolph, the director of Rosemont Hospital. He was a tall, heavyset man in his late fifties.

"It's nice to see Carson Drew's daughter on our volunteer staff," he said, greeting Nancy.

The lawyer was on the board of the hospital and a personal friend of Dr. Randolph.

"I suppose you've heard about your amnesia patient," Nancy said.

"Of course. He's the most exciting thing that's happened around here all week!" the man replied. "Not that it's so exciting for him, poor guy. We called Chief McGinnis to see if anyone on the police department's list of missing persons fits his description."

"What did you find out?" George asked.

"Absolutely nothing. The police wanted to know if Cliff had been physically assaulted," Dr. Randolph went on. "But there was no evidence of that, according to Dr. Anderson."

"In other words," Bess said, "there's no reason for the police to get involved—"

"Yet," Nancy added in a serious tone.

"Why, what do you mean?" Dr. Randolph replied.

The girl told him about the bearded stranger,

19

his accusation, and her discovery of the ring. "At the moment, it's our only clue to Cliff's identity," she said, "and I'd like to study it some more."

"Good idea, Nancy."

Promising to keep the man posted on all developments, she and her friends stepped out into the hallway.

"When I signed on as a volunteer, I was asked to help distribute flowers, so I'll do that now," the young detective told Bess and George. "Maybe we ought to put our heads together later."

"Call us when you get home," George said.

Nancy immediately headed for the main lobby, where several colorful floral arrangements were displayed on a counter.

"These are for the third floor, and this one's for the sixth," the clerk told Nancy.

She fastened her eyes on the latter in surprise. The card was marked TOMMY JOHNSON. Was it her neighborhood friend? Curious, she went to Pediatrics on the sixth floor first. The boy's mother was just emerging from his room.

"Mrs. Johnson!" Nancy cried.

Without questioning Nancy's presence at Rosemont, the woman blurted out her story.

20

"Tommy was riding his bicycle when a car cut in front of him. He and the bike toppled over. He hit his head on the curb and twisted his leg—broke it in two places."

Nancy winced at the thought. "Oh, how terrible! Has he been operated on yet?"

"No, but he will be this afternoon."

"These are for Tommy," Nancy said, indicating the small basket of flowers.

She stepped into the room, where the shade was pulled low to keep out the bright sun. Tommy, a small bandage over one eyebrow, was sleeping quietly. He did not move until Nancy placed the flowers next to him. Then his eyes opened slowly.

"Hi, Nancy," the boy said. "Did you come to visit me?"

"I sure did," the girl replied cheerfully.

She touched his cheek gently as an orderly appeared. "We must get him ready now," the young man said, signaling the girl to leave.

Mrs. Johnson had remained outside the door, waiting to speak to her.

"Did anyone see the car?" Nancy asked the woman.

Tommy's mother shook her head. "I don't think so, but I'm not sure," she said. "It hap-

pened on the corner of Hathaway Street and
Elm Avenue."

Nancy squeezed Mrs. Johnson's arm as she
promised to help find the hit-and-run driver.
At her first opportunity, she would make a
trip to police headquarters.

"Now I have two reasons to go," Nancy said
without explaining further.

She said good-bye and headed for the fifth
floor to speak with Lisa. To her surprise, the
young woman had gone off duty.

That's strange, Nancy thought. I'm positive
she was supposed to work until five o'clock. I
hope she took care of Cliff's ring for him.

Instantly, the girl detective returned to the
main floor and the admitting office, where she
inquired about the valuable piece.

"One moment," the clerk said, and stepped
into the inner office, shortly reappearing
empty-handed. "I can find no notation about
the deposit of a ring from Room 502, and it's not
in the safe."

"Are you positive?" Nancy inquired.

"Quite," the woman bristled.

What had happened to Cliff's ring? Nancy
wondered anxiously. And where was Lisa?

As quickly as she could, Nancy checked out of the hospital and headed for Lisa's home. It was near Hathaway Street, where Tommy's accident had occurred. When Nancy reached the busy intersection at Elm Avenue, she noticed a tall, thin man with a briefcase enter a jewelry store. He was wearing a business suit and a white silk turban that offset his brown face and fine Indian features. But of even more interest was the man running after him. It was the bearded stranger who had attacked Cliff!

I have to talk to him! Nancy said to herself.

She swung her car into a space halfway down the street, pushed a coin into the meter, and ran toward the shop. She paused before entering.

Lisa! she gulped when she saw the girl, who was talking with the businessman and the shopkeeper. Where was the other man? Had he seen Nancy coming and disappeared?

She was tempted to explore the alley next to the store, but the scene inside was more fascinating. Lisa was showing Cliff's ring to the shopkeeper. Suddenly, he left the counter, and the stranger pocketed the ring. He hurried to the door, which Nancy flung open with such force that he slipped off balance.

"You took that young woman's ring," Nancy accused, alerting both Lisa and the shopkeeper.

Instantly, the man shoved Nancy against the counter. He grabbed the door, ready to dart outside, but the shopkeeper and Lisa rushed forward, tackling him. Nancy dived into his coat pocket and quickly retrieved the ring.

"Let go of me!" the man shouted, unaware that the valuable trinket had been removed.

He tore away from the group and ran across the street to a bus that had stopped at the corner.

"We'll catch him!" Nancy exclaimed.

Without another word, Lisa hurried after her friend to Nancy's car. As quickly as she could, Nancy pulled around in the opposite direction. The bus was several stoplights away from her.

"Why didn't you put Cliff's ring into the hospital safe?" Nancy asked as they sped forward.

"I meant to, but Cliff suggested I take it to a local jeweler—to find out more about it. Next thing I knew, that man in the turban was standing there, asking all sorts of questions."

By now, Nancy's car had caught up to the bus at a bus stop, where several people debarked. She signaled to the driver to wait.

"What do you want?" the man shouted through his window. "I've got a lot of people to let off."

"One of them tried to rob us," Lisa called back.

Before Nancy could park, her friend had jumped out of the car and raced to the policeman on the corner, leading him quickly to the bus. When the last of several passengers had stepped off, Lisa and the officer jumped on board. There were only a few people left, and the man in the turban was not among them!

3

Mean Accusation

Through her rearview mirror, Nancy watched Lisa and the policeman step off the bus without the Indian. The girl detective immediately switched on her hazard lights, leaving the car double-parked, and leaped out.

"What happened?" she asked, hurrying toward them.

"I don't know. He must have sneaked off without our seeing him," Lisa replied.

The officer listened to the girls' story while Nancy displayed Cliff's ring. "Lucky you were on the scene, Nancy Drew," he complimented her.

Nancy's reputation as a keen detective was well-known to the police of River Heights.

"I was planning to see Chief McGinnis tomorrow," Nancy said. "But maybe Lisa and I ought to go to headquarters now."

"Good idea," the policeman grinned, "especially since I don't want to tow your car away."

The girls glanced in the direction of Nancy's flashing rear lights. She suddenly realized she had double-parked next to a patrol car!

"Sorry," she said sheepishly.

When the pair reached the station, Nancy explained that she had two important matters to discuss with the chief. One related to the identity of a local amnesia patient who had been assaulted in the hospital. The other had to do with the driver of a car that had nearly run down Tommy Johnson.

"I know about both cases," Chief McGinnis said, "but I have no lead on the first and only a very slim one on the second."

Nancy gave a description of the bearded man.

"I've seen him twice now," she said. "The first time he took off in a tan-colored car with a blue racing stripe on the trunk."

"What's the license number?"

Nancy shrugged. "I couldn't see it."

The chief hunched forward on his elbows and shook his head thoughtfully.

27

"Do you have any idea whom it belongs to?" Nancy asked.

"Yes, I think so. Of course, I can't be absolutely positive, but—"

"But what?"

"It sounds like the same car that caused the Johnson boy's accident."

Nancy was stunned into silence as her mind raced over the events of the afternoon. What was the connection between the Indian businessman and the bearded stranger?

"I have a hunch the bearded man may be the driver we're looking for!" Nancy exclaimed.

"You could be right," Chief McGinnis said. "I'll let you know if anything definite turns up on either of those men."

Nancy promised to reciprocate and said good-bye. As the girls headed for Lisa's house, the young nurse suggested that Nancy keep the ring.

"It'll be safer with you," Lisa insisted, adding an apology for what had occurred earlier. "I should have put it in the hospital safe."

"Just be glad we have it," Nancy smiled. "Besides, your visit to the jewelry shop turned up an interesting character."

"And some interesting information," Lisa

said. "This is the first chance I've had to tell you what Mr. Jhaveri, the jeweler, said about the ring. He's quite an expert on foreign jewelry, and he believes the design is Asiatic.

"The other man disagreed, however. He kept saying the ring was Middle Eastern. That's when Mr. Jhaveri said he would show me some pictures as proof."

"And that's when the Indian businessman tried to steal the ring," Nancy put in.

"Exactly."

"He didn't count on Nancy Drew," Lisa added, causing a blush of crimson to cross her friend's face.

They pulled up in front of the Scotti home and Lisa opened the car door instantly.

"I promised Mom I'd cook dinner tonight, so I'd better run," she said. "Thanks a lot. See you tomorrow."

Nancy said good-bye, all the while thinking about the scene in the jewelry shop. She was tempted to return there, but a glance at her watch told her she was more than an hour late for dinner.

Hannah is probably worried about me, Nancy thought. I can just imagine the phone calls she must have made to the hospital.

The girl pressed down on the accelerator, watching the speedometer needle waver just under the speed limit. Rush-hour traffic had eased up, and she found herself in the driveway of the Drew home within fifteen minutes. Mrs. Gruen opened the door with a mixture of disapproval and relief on her face.

"I'm sorry," Nancy said, hugging the woman. "I was on my way home when—"

"You caught two robbers, found three clues, and went to see Chief McGinnis," Hannah replied, unable to keep from smiling.

"How did you guess?"

"Because I know you. That's how." The housekeeper grinned.

Before Nancy said another word, she raced upstairs to freshen up. The aroma of home-baked peach pie trailed after her, speeding her back to the dining room table where her father was already seated.

"Do I have lots of news!" Nancy said excitedly.

Carson Drew, a distinguished-looking man in his forties, did not respond immediately. Nancy thought he seemed disturbed.

"Is something wrong, Dad?"

"Oh, no," he answered quickly.

"Sure?"

"Sure."

"I really am sorry about being late."

Her father merely nodded as he took a sip of water. "Bring me up to date on what happened today," he said at last.

Despite her eagerness to tell him, she could not help being distracted by Mr. Drew's sullen manner. Nonetheless, she revealed her encounters at the hospital, the discovery of the ring, and Tommy Johnson's accident.

"How terrible!" Hannah commented when the girl finished speaking.

For the first time since dinner began, Mr. Drew's expression was also animated. He asked several questions, then lapsed into silence until he rose from the table.

"Let's go into the living room, Nancy," he said.

What was on her father's mind? Nancy wondered in puzzlement. She sank into the deep, soft cushions of the chair by the fireplace and waited anxiously.

"I really don't know how to say this," Mr. Drew said slowly.

"Does it have to do with the music festival?"

"In a way, yes." Her father paused. "You'll have to stop doing your detective work for a while."

Nancy blinked in disbelief. "But why? What have I done?"

"Oh, *you* haven't done anything wrong. The townspeople of Castleton think *I* have."

"You've lost me, Dad."

"As I told you yesterday, I've been handling negotiations for the River Heights festival on behalf of River Heights."

"Negotiations between the city and the different performing groups who are appearing here this summer," Nancy put in.

"That's right," her father replied. "Well, I've been accused of theft."

"Theft?" Nancy repeated in utter astonishment. "That's absolutely crazy."

"Castleton claims that River Heights has deliberately stolen one of the theater companies it booked for its own outdoor pavilion."

"I still don't understand."

"It's very simple, dear. The Jansen Music Theater Company was scheduled to perform at the Castleton Theater, but Jansen canceled out on Castleton in favor of River Heights. The town council of Castleton thinks I'm responsible for the last-minute switch." Mr. Drew interrupted himself, laughing nervously. "It just isn't true, but I can't seem to convince anyone, including the mayor of River Heights!"

"But he's your friend, Dad."

"He is, but he's also in an awkward situation with Castleton, since both communities have been working together on some environmental issues."

Nancy took a deep breath. "I'll help you," she said.

"No, Nancy, I think it's better if you don't. A number of unexplained things have happened to the Jansen troupe, and I'm afraid something could happen to you."

"You know I can take care of myself," Nancy pleaded.

"I would feel better if you just contented yourself with the amnesia patient."

The firmness in his voice told Nancy she ought not to push him on the subject.

It's the first time Dad has ever told me to quit on something before I even started, Nancy said to herself.

Worse than that, her own father needed her help, but would not accept it!

4

Suspect?

"Nancy, I don't want you to worry about me or the festival," Mr. Drew said.

"But Dad—"

He raised his hand as if he didn't want to hear another word.

"I have two complimentary tickets to the festival tomorrow evening. Perhaps you'd like to take Ned."

Nancy's face lit up into a smile immediately.

"Promise me, though, you'll just enjoy the performance. No investigating, okay?"

"Whatever you say, Dad."

She leaped out of her chair to call her friend, Ned Nickerson, who was home on vacation from

Emerson College. At first Nancy was tempted to mention her father's predicament, but she refrained as Mr. Drew strode past her.

Instead, she conveyed the invitation, adding in a whisper, "I have a lot to tell you, too."

"In that case," Ned said, "how can I resist?"

It was decided that he would stop by for Nancy at seven-thirty the next evening. In the meantime, she had several things to discuss with Bess and George.

"Hello. Is George there?" Nancy said, after dialing the number of the Fayne household.

To her surprise, the girl was not home.

Maybe she went to see Bess, Nancy surmised. She was about to call the Marvin number when the doorbell rang.

"I'll get it," Nancy announced, dropping the receiver.

It was the two cousins.

"When we didn't hear from you, we figured something must've happened," Bess said.

"Right?" George asked.

"Right," Nancy said. "Come on in."

While she cut pieces of Hannah's peach pie for each girl, she told them everything that had occurred after they left Rosemont Hospital.

"Fortunately, I still have Cliff's ring," Nancy concluded, excusing herself to get it.

When she returned to the kitchen, she was also holding her magnifying glass. The trio took turns examining the ring. On close inspection, they saw that the intricate design consisted of finely intertwined water lilies. Inside the band was a well-worn initial, together with an indistinct figure standing on a flower. To the untrained eye, they could pass for mere scratches.

"I can't figure out what the letter is," Bess said. "Can you?"

"I'm not sure, but it looks like 'P,'" Nancy said. "Lisa said Mr. Jhaveri was about to show her a book when the businessman took the ring."

"Maybe we should go to the store tomorrow," George suggested.

"I was just thinking the same thing," Nancy said.

That night, Nancy slept uneasily as the ring tossed through her dreams. Someone on the stage of the River Heights Theater was throwing it toward her, but she couldn't catch it because of an imaginary rope that held her arms back.

"Nancy . . . Nancy," a voice was calling.

The girl mumbled back into her pillow as the shade on her window snapped open and sunlight poured across the room.

"Nancy, dear, it's after nine."

The young detective pulled the bedsheet over her head while Hannah tickled her foot.

"Time to rise and shine. Bess and George are waiting for you downstairs."

"Oh, my goodness," Nancy cried, bolting out of bed. "They're here already?"

After a quick shower, she slipped into a skirt and blouse, put Cliff's ring in her shoulder bag, and hurried to the dining room, where a glass of orange juice awaited her.

"Didn't we say nine o'clock?" George asked.

Nancy nodded. "I overslept," she said, gulping down the juice.

"Don't drink so fast, Nancy," Hannah scolded. "You'll get indigestion."

Despite the warning, Nancy hurried through breakfast, explaining that she had several things to do.

"I promised to be at the hospital for a couple of hours at least," she said. "Now that I'm running so late, maybe you ought to see Mr. Jhaveri without me."

"Are you sure?" Bess asked.

"Yes. Besides, I want to check on how Tommy is and make a few inquiries at the hospital."

"What about the ring?" George replied. "Shall we take it with us?"

"Definitely," Nancy said. "When you're done at the store, then please bring it to Rosemont."

While Nancy headed for the hospital, Bess and George went downtown. To their delight, Mr. Jhaveri remembered the unusual ring and was more than willing to discuss it.

"I didn't have a chance to show my book to your friend," he said, "but I will show it to you. Do you have time?"

"Oh yes," George replied eagerly.

"I will only be a moment," the proprietor said, disappearing into the anteroom behind the main counter.

For an instant, the cousins sensed that someone was watching them, but when they glanced toward the front window, no one was there.

"We're just being overly suspicious," Bess whispered.

Mr. Jhaveri returned holding a large book. "There are many wonderful stories in here about unusual pieces of jewelry and their owners." He leafed through the pages, stopping now and then to show photographs of fantastic jewels—rubies, diamonds, and emeralds cut in various shapes.

"Ah, here it is," he said at last. "The Maharajah Prithviraj of Lakshmipur."

Bess and George giggled as they looked at the roly-poly man whose face was as round as Hannah's peach pie. He wore a loose-fitting robe that concealed his rotund figure, and on every finger except one was an exquisite ring.

"It seems that the maharajah had a passion for water lilies," Mr. Jhaveri said. "They grew profusely in his garden pool—"

"And decorated his linen, silver, and jewelry," Bess said, reading the caption under the picture.

Was it possible that Cliff's ring had once belonged to the maharajah? the girls wondered. But, if so, how had it traveled from India to the United States?

The bell on the front door jingled suddenly, and the girls stared at the bearded man who entered. Was he the same person Nancy had chased out of Rosemont Hospital?

George quickly dropped the ring into her purse and shut the book.

40

"Are you finished with it?" Mr. Jhaveri asked politely.

"Yes, thank you," George said, trying to conceal her nervousness. She nudged Bess to leave. "We must be on our way, but I'm sure we'll be back."

"Don't hurry on my account," the bearded customer said. "I'm just browsing."

The girls did not bother to reply, but hurried to their car.

"Maybe we should've stayed around to check that guy out," Bess said.

"And risk having him hear something about the ring?" George replied. "No, ma'am."

She started the car, then noticed that the jeweler had emerged from his store. The bearded man was with him.

"Don't go yet, miss!" Mr. Jhaveri was shouting at the girls. "Please—come back!"

"What should we do?" Bess gasped. Her heart pounded nervously as the stranger raced toward them.

5

Untimely Ruse

"I'm positive that man is after Cliff's ring!" Bess exclaimed fearfully.

"Just keep cool," George said, turning off the ignition.

By now, the bearded man was standing next to the girl's car.

"I am Dr. DeNiro, the anthropologist," he introduced himself.

George recognized the name immediately. Dr. DeNiro was a professor at Oberon College, a local university and had recently returned from field work in Asia. An article about him had appeared in the last issue of the *River Heights Gazette*.

"I'm George Fayne, and this is my cousin, Bess Marvin," George said.

"How do you do?"

Bess smiled sweetly, lifting her eyes to the thin, almost invisible scar that traveled down the man's cheek and disappeared under the ragged beard.

"We're sort of in a hurry," George said.

"Well, I don't want to hold you up, but—uh," the man stumbled, "I am interested in the ring you showed Mr. Jhaveri."

The cousins remained silent, waiting for him to go on.

"May I see it?" Dr. DeNiro said.

George hesitated, then dug into her purse, as earlier suspicions were replaced by curiosity. Perhaps the professor could provide some clues to Cliff's identity!

"Here you are," the girl said, handing the ring to him.

He studied it intently, turning it over several times.

"I have been doing some research on the area of India where this was made," the man said. "With your permission, I would like to photograph the ring. May I?"

"It doesn't belong to us," Bess replied.

"Oh, I see. Well, in that case, could you put me in touch with the owner?"

The girls paused.

"Perhaps you could give me his name and telephone number," Dr. DeNiro continued.

"He's in the hospital," George said. Her mind was racing as it occurred to her that Nancy might wish to speak with the professor as well. "We're on our way to Rosemont Hospital now. Would you like to ride over there with us?"

The man checked his watch. "Oh," he gasped, "I'm twenty minutes late for my appointment. I'll have to call you."

With that, he sped across the street to a parking lot, leaving the girls in complete bafflement.

"The ring! He's got the ring!" George cried. She leaped out of her car and darted after the man, shouting his name at the top of her lungs. But he was already pulling out of the lot.

"What happened?" Bess asked when her cousin returned.

"He's gone."

"And so is Cliff's ring," Bess said. "We have to get it back before we see Nancy again."

George agreed and suggested that they go to Oberon College.

"Maybe we'll catch him on the way to class," Bess said hopefully.

The girls located his office in an old stone building near the student center. A note was tacked on the door: HOURS 1:30–3:00 P.M.

"He should be here in a few minutes," George observed with a sigh of relief.

The wait, however, seemed interminable, as a stream of students carrying notebooks filed through the corridor and stopped outside an instructor's door at the far end.

"Where is he?" Bess asked impatiently.

Then, as if in reply, the large, wooden, entrance door swung open and a young, brown-haired man, neatly dressed in a striped shirt and khaki pants, strode toward them.

"May I help you?" he asked, pulling out a key.

"We're looking for Dr. DeNiro," George said.

"You've found him." The beardless man grinned. "Are you registering for one of my courses?"

His listeners stared at him completely dumbfounded.

"Is something wrong?" the instructor asked.

"No . . . I mean, yes," Bess said. "Do you have a brother who teaches here?"

"No," he chuckled, "but I'm sure my department head would be pleased if I did. I've been away from campus for almost a month."

The realization that Cliff's ring was now in the possession of an unknown stranger made both girls shudder. They had been duped!

Instantly, George asked, "Are you missing any personal identification—driver's license, credit cards, anything like that?"

"No, not that I know of. Why?"

George explained about their encounter with the man at the jewelery shop.

"He said he was you!" Bess exclaimed.

"Me?"

By now, the young man had opened his office and invited the cousins to sit down.

"He said he was doing some research on India and wanted to photograph the ring we gave him," George explained.

"Well, it's true I am working on a government project related to India, but it hasn't been publicized." He paused for a long moment. "I do wonder, though, why someone would pretend to be me."

"All we know is that the ring may have belonged to a maharajah."

The young man slid back in his chair, staring at the girls, yet past them.

"It's possible," he said, "that the fellow expects to gain access to information I'm after."

"What kind of information?" Bess inquired.

"I'm afraid I can't tell you."

She and George concluded that the professor must be involved in a highly confidential mission. The question was, Did the ring figure into it, and if so, how?

Before they could discuss it further, a student appeared at the door. She was holding several notebooks.

"I may need to talk with you both again," Dr. DeNiro said, signaling the cousins to leave.

"And vice versa," George said. She jotted down her phone number. "Will you be here tomorrow?"

"Yes, I have a course in the morning and another one in the afternoon."

The cousins said good-bye and hurried to the car.

"This whole thing is getting pretty weird," Bess commented.

"I'm beginning to think Cliff lost his memory on purpose," George said.

"What? You think he's faking?" Bess replied. "I don't believe it."

"I don't either, really, but that doesn't mean it isn't possible. After all, he could be in serious trouble and need a place to hide out."

"I can think of nicer places than a hospital," Bess remarked.

"True, but maybe he was trying to escape when he fell. The next thing he knew he was in the hospital. Since he didn't want anyone to know who or where he was, he conveniently forgot his name."

"I still don't believe it."

"Well, it's just a thought," George replied.

The girls said little else until they reached Rosemont, where they went to Cliff's room promptly. A curtain had been pulled around his bed and Lisa was talking with a doctor.

"Where's Nancy?" Bess asked when Lisa had finished her conversation.

"She went to see Dr. Anderson," Lisa said with evident concern in her voice.

The cousins glanced at the curtain.

"Is Cliff all right?"

"Yes, he is now," the nurse replied. "But an hour ago he started screaming and choking."

Had the bearded stranger returned to attack Cliff again? the girls wondered.

6

Harpist's Predicament

"What happened?" Bess asked anxiously.

"Did that bearded guy—" George started to say when Nancy dashed toward them.

"Cliff had a terrible nightmare," she said, pulling the girls away from the young man's door.

"Oh, thank goodness it wasn't anything more serious than that," Bess said.

"Even so, Cliff needs to be in a different environment," Nancy remarked. "Dr. Anderson agrees."

"Is Cliff well enough to be moved?" George asked Lisa.

"That's up to the doctor."

"Even if he can leave," Bess said, "where would he go?"

"To my house," Nancy said. "Hannah will see that he eats three full meals every day—"

"If that doesn't bring back his memory, nothing will!" Bess laughed.

"And speaking of losing things," Nancy said, suddenly remembering the girls' mission downtown, "do you have Cliff's ring?"

The cousins gulped. That was the inevitable question they had been dreading.

"No, I'm afraid not," George said. She explained all that had happened, ending with their visit to Oberon College.

Nancy listened in shock. "That was our only clue to Cliff's identity," she said anxiously.

"I know it doesn't help to say we're sorry," Bess replied.

"But we are. We really are," George added.

Nancy slipped her arms around the girls' shoulders. "Don't worry about it. You're not easily fooled, so the impersonator must be a pretty slick character," she said, catching sight of Cliff's doctor down the hallway. "Excuse me a moment. I must talk to Dr. Anderson."

She hurried toward him, and after several minutes of conversation, rejoined her friends.

"He wants to keep Cliff here until after lunch tomorrow," she announced, "but after that,

Cliff will belong to the Drew family!"

"I wonder how Ned will feel about that," George mumbled.

"There isn't a jealous bone in Ned's body," Nancy replied confidently. "I'll tell him everything tonight."

But when she reached home later that afternoon, she admitted she wasn't only worried about the whereabouts of Cliff's ring. She was also reconsidering the wisdom of her new plan. After all, Cliff was only a few years older than Ned, and Ned had often complained that she spent less time with him than solving mysteries. The fact that this one happens to involve a young, handsome man could be the last straw, Nancy thought.

Her father, however, disagreed with her conclusion. "After all, our house probably is the safest place for Cliff," he said.

So when Ned arrived, Nancy announced her news cheerfully.

"Is something wrong?" she asked him, watching his buoyant smile shrink.

Ned shook his head. "We're running late," he said, "and I don't want to break any speed limits on the way to the theater."

"'Bye, everybody," Nancy said as they darted

to Ned's car. As she buckled her seat belt, she remarked, "Dad thinks Cliff will be much better off at our house than in the hospital."

"Guess so," Ned answered crisply.

He said little else, however, until they reached the theater, where several neighbors of the Drews greeted Nancy. Other townspeople, mostly members of the municipal board, stared coldly at her.

"Is it my imagination," Ned said, "or did the mayor and his wife just snub you?"

"Yes, they did," Nancy replied, feeling immediately uncomfortable. "But if you noticed, I smiled at them anyway. I'll explain later."

As the couple walked down to the front of the hall, they heard a rising murmur behind them. The mayor's wife was adjusting her summer shawl and leaning forward to talk to a councilman's wife. She, in turn, hissed back in a loud whisper. Nancy knew they were talking about her father.

"Can't you tell me what's going on now?" Ned said in a low voice.

"No—" was all the girl could say as musicians filed onstage.

When they were seated, a gray-haired man

with a baton went quickly to the podium, causing a round of applause that grew louder as a young, red-haired woman took her place at the gleaming harp downstage.

Ned glanced at the program. The first piece featuring Angela Pruett, the harp soloist, was "Introduction and Allegro" by Maurice Ravel.

"This is going to be even more interesting than I thought," Ned teased Nancy.

When the harpist began to play, however, the strings of the instrument squawked like a flock of birds, each one singing off-key!

"What's going on?" Ned whispered to Nancy.

"I don't know," she said, "and apparently no one on stage does either."

The orchestra stopped playing as the conductor and harpist exchanged puzzled frowns and a few words.

"We are terribly sorry, ladies and gentlemen," the conductor announced to the audience, "but Miss Pruett's harp seems to be badly out of tune. We will continue our program with the next selection and perform 'Introduction and Allegro' after intermission."

Nancy leaned toward Ned. "Strange, very

strange," she said. "That instrument should have been tuned and checked before the concert began."

"Maybe someone tampered with it," Ned replied mysteriously.

That's exactly what Nancy was thinking. But why would anyone want to ruin the performance?

She was tempted to go backstage during intermission, but decided to wait until the end of the performance. To her delight, the rest of it went beautifully and uneventfully.

"I really enjoyed it," Ned told Nancy as her eyes drifted to the musicians leaving the stage.

"That makes me very happy," she replied, suddenly grabbing Ned's hand.

"Gee, if I knew that's all I had to say—"

"C'mon, let's go," Nancy interrupted quickly. "I want to talk to Miss Pruett."

Ned shook his head disconsolately. "And I thought this was going to be a detective-less evening," he mumbled.

Nancy disregarded the comment as she asked an usher where the stage entrance was.

"Outside and to the left," was the answer.

Without another word, the couple hurried toward the exit. Nancy did not even pay attention to the stares from the mayor and his wife as she passed in front of them. A minute or two more, and she and Ned were climbing a flight of steps to the musicians' room.

"Miss Pruett!" Nancy called out to the young woman when she finally emerged.

The harpist glanced at Nancy with a fearful look in her eyes. "Yes?" she replied.

"I'm Nancy Drew, and this is my friend, Ned Nickerson—"

Noticing the programs in their hands, she asked, "Did you wish an autograph?"

"No—I mean, yes," Ned replied, broadening his smile. He handed her a pen.

The young woman quickly scrawled her name. "You have lovely handwriting," Nancy said.

Nonetheless, she observed a certain stiffness in the curve of the letters. Perhaps the performance had exhausted her, or, Nancy wondered, was she suffering from the strain of what had occurred earlier?

"Miss Pruett, I would like to ask you a few questions, if I may—about—" Nancy began.

"About the humiliating thing that happened to me?" the young woman replied, tears forming in her eyes. "There was no excuse—none!"

Nancy explained that she was an amateur detective who had a particular interest in the music festival because of her father's association with it.

"It seems to us that someone must've deliberately turned all the pegs on your harp," Ned declared.

Miss Pruett blinked her eyes as if trying to push the whole episode out of her mind.

"I appreciate your concern," she said abruptly, "but I'd rather not talk about it now, if you don't mind."

"Will you be here tomorrow?" Nancy inquired.

"Yes, but I can't stay after the performance," the harpist said, adding nervously, "I have some errands to do. Now please excuse me. I must go."

"But—" Nancy said, hoping to persuade her into granting an appointment.

The young woman walked away, however, and disappeared through a door at the end of the hall.

"She obviously doesn't want our help," Ned remarked.

"I have a hunch, though, that she really needs it," Nancy replied.

7

The Sister's Story

"Speaking of help," Ned said, "I could use some myself."

"You could?" Nancy replied, suddenly shifting her eyes to his.

He sighed, allowing the bewildered expression on Nancy's face to grow into curiosity.

"Don't keep me in suspense, Ned," the girl detective said as they headed for the car.

But the boy was savoring the attention. "I'd rather you tell me all your news." Ned chuckled.

"That's not a fair answer," Nancy said, somewhat hurt. "After all, we're supposed to be friends, and you're practically saying you don't want my help."

"I didn't say that at all," Ned retorted, suddenly wishing he had never started the conversation.

Nancy, in turn, settled into silence until they reached the newly opened diner.

"You might as well have said it," she murmured finally.

"And you're making a mountain out of a molehill," Ned said, turning off the ignition.

The girl suddenly buried her face in her hands. "I'm sorry," she said. "I guess I just overreacted because of Dad."

"I don't understand," Ned said. "What do I have to do with your father?"

"You don't. It's just that he doesn't want me to help him either."

"Let's go inside and order something," Ned suggested. "Then you can tell me everything."

"Okay," Nancy replied in a soft voice, and for a few moments she forgot her troubles as they entered the diner.

Counters and booths glistened against panels of beveled mirrors, and a string of colorful Tiffany lamps hung from the ceiling, transporting the couple to a bygone era.

"Some place," Ned remarked as they slid into a booth.

"You can say that again," Nancy said, opening the tall menu that had been handed to her.

Her eyes traveled down the length of unusual fare. "How about a Tango Fandango?" She giggled. "That's only five scoops of ice cream with melba sauce, coconut, chopped nuts, raisins, and whipped cream!"

When the waitress came to take their orders, however, both settled for simple hot fudge sundaes and tea.

Nancy then related the conversation she had had with her father earlier in the evening.

"But your dad would never do anything underhanded," Ned said, when Nancy finished talking.

"He mentioned that things had been happening to the Jansen troupe. He didn't say what, though."

"He also told you not to get involved."

Nancy lowered her eyes away from Ned as he continued to look at her. He had never seen the girl so obviously distraught.

"I just can't let people say such terrible things about Dad," she said. "I know he wants me to stay out of it, but I can't."

As she spoke, the waitress brought the sundaes. Nancy spooned a bit of the mountainous whipped cream into her cup, stirring it more than necessary.

"Listen, Nancy, if you want me to help you in any way," Ned said, "I will. But I'd also like to say I don't think you ought to go against your father's wishes."

"Well, Dad said he didn't want anything to happen to me. That was his main concern," Nancy pointed out. "But if you're with me, I'm bound to be all right."

The young collegian blushed and dug his spoon deeper into the ice cream, catching some of the fudge sauce that floated in the bowl.

When they were almost finished, Nancy grinned mysteriously. "You said you needed help on something," she began to say.

"Oh, yeah—well, it's nothing really," Ned stumbled in embarrassment. "I was just trying to send a little of your attention my way."

"Oh, I see," Nancy said as her companion went on.

"Now that we have this big investigation ahead of us, I'll be too busy to feel sorry for myself."

"Have I been that neglectful?" Nancy asked sheepishly.

The young man smiled in response, but

chose not to pursue the subject. It was after eleven o'clock, and he suggested they leave. When they reached the Drew home, however, they were surprised to see a visitor in the light of the living room window.

"It's Angela Pruett, and she's talking to Dad!" Nancy exclaimed.

She and Ned darted toward the front door that had been left unlocked. They stepped inside, aware of a sudden hush in the conversation.

"Is that you, Nancy?" Mr. Drew called out.

"And Ned," she replied, walking into the room. She smiled pleasantly at the harpist.

"I gather you all met at the performance this evening," the attorney commented.

"I was hoping we would see you again," Nancy told the harpist.

The musician leaned back in her chair and closed her eyes momentarily.

"Miss Pruett has been trying to find her sister for several days," Mr. Drew revealed. "It seems she went on some sort of spiritual retreat last weekend, but never returned."

"Where was the retreat being held?" Nancy inquired.

"Somewhere in the hills outside of River

Heights," the harpist replied. "I don't know exactly. Phyllis is very interested in Transcendental Meditation."

"We didn't realize you were from River Heights, Miss Pruett," Ned commented.

"I'm not. And please call me Angela," the harpist said. "As I told your father, Nancy, I took the festival job because I wanted to see my sister again. She ran away from home last year, and it was only a month ago that she wrote to me. She begged me, though, not to tell anyone where she was.

"The minute I had her address, I scouted around for some way to spend the summer here. Of course, I was hoping to convince her to come home before I left River Heights. She's not quite seventeen yet."

"Has she been living at the retreat?" Nancy asked.

"No. According to her letter, she took a room in someone's house. I believe it belonged to their son, but he's away at school now. I called Mrs. Flannery the minute I arrived. She said that Phyllis hadn't been home all weekend.

"I contacted the police, but they don't have any leads," Angela Pruett went on. "When I met you tonight, I realized that maybe I needed to hire a private detective, and I was wondering—"

Nancy's face broke into a soft smile. "I'm afraid you can't hire me, Angela," she said.

"Then you won't help me?"

"On the contrary. I will help you, but I won't if you insist upon paying me."

"We'll find your sister," Ned said confidently.

"That's right," Nancy joined in, slipping her arm into his. "We'll start tomorrow."

But as she made the commitment, she thought of Cliff, the missing ring, her hospital work, and Tommy Johnson. Somehow, she would have to make time for everything!

Ned called her early in the morning. "What's our schedule today?" he asked cheerfully. "I mean, are you ready for a hike in the hills of River Heights?"

Nancy laughed. "Maybe after I hike the halls of Rosemont Hospital!" she said. "I'm supposed to bring Cliff home—to our house, that is."

There was dead silence at the other end of the line, then Ned cleared his throat. "Well, when would that be?" he asked.

"Oh, probably around one o'clock."

In the back of Nancy's mind was a visit to Dr. DeNiro's office at Oberon College. But she refrained from mentioning it, since she would have to find out the professor's schedule before making an appointment to see him.

"Ned, would you like to come by about two?" Nancy said.

"Okay," he said with renewed enthusiasm. "For a minute there, I thought you were going to back out on our plans for today."

"Me? Never!" she said. "See you later." She then called Bess and George to fill them in on the events of the night before.

Their mothers, they said, were going shopping and had invited the girls to accompany them.

"I didn't want to disappoint Mom," Bess said. "Neither did George. But if you need us—"

"Don't give it a second thought," Nancy insisted. She told them of her plans for the day, adding that by the end of it she would be in touch again. "That is, unless Ned and I get lost!"

The morning at the hospital seemed to fly. Tommy Johnson had made considerable progress, and in between small errands, Nancy would stop in to see him. On her last visit, she brought him a big picture book filled with riddles.

"These are funny, Nancy," the young patient said, giggling at the pictures.

"Hickory dickory dock," Nancy said, pointing to the first one, "the mouse ran up the clock. The clock struck one and down he came. Hickory dickory dock."

"What time is it now?" Tommy asked.

"It's not quite twelve-thirty."

"Then the mouse has thirty minutes to go," he laughed.

"And so do I," Nancy said, ruffling the boy's hair. "I'll see you tomorrow."

She darted down the corridor and took the elevator to Cliff's floor. He had recovered from the episode of the day before and was fully dressed, waiting for someone to bring a wheelchair in which to take him downstairs.

"I'm so grateful to you," he said, "but I hope this won't be an imposition on you and your father."

"Nonsense," Nancy remarked. "You need to be in a different environment."

"I need some fresh air, too," he said, as the

pungent odor of antiseptics floated down the hall.

The girl detective had deliberately not said anything about the Drews' concern for the young man's safety. Why compound his anxiety? she thought.

When they finally arrived at the Drew house, Cliff seemed almost happy. Although he still felt somewhat weak, he greeted Hannah enthusiastically. She and Nancy showed him to his room, where he sank into a chair.

"You rest now until dinner," the housekeeper suggested, closing the door quietly.

Nancy briefly explained that she would be gone most of the afternoon but would make certain to be back before six.

"Where have I heard that before?" Hannah said.

"From me, of course." Nancy grinned.

She changed into her oldest jeans and a long-sleeved shirt, then answered a call from Angela Pruett, who was just leaving for a performance.

"Ned's coming over soon and we're going to try to find that retreat," Nancy told her.

"Then I'm glad I caught you. One thing I did

today was to reread Phyllis's letter. She described the retreat a little bit. Apparently it's near a large la—"

Suddenly the line went dead. They had been cut off! Nancy clicked the receiver several times, but nothing happened. She redialed, but got only a busy signal.

"I'll call the operator, she said to herself, and dialed zero.

"I will place the call for you and credit your previous call," the operator said in a matter-of-fact tone. "We regret the inconvenience."

Nancy hung on the phone, anxiously waiting to hear Angela's voice again.

"I am sorry." It was the operator again. "That number is out of order."

Now what? Nancy wondered. She had just missed hearing possible clues to the location of the retreat!

8

Tangled Trail

As Nancy stood by the telephone in the Drew hallway, her eyes darted to the figure hurrying up the driveway. She pulled open the door and let the warm breeze sweep inside.

"Hi, Ned!" Nancy cried. The glaze of disappointment disappeared from her face temporarily.

"All set?" he replied with a quick glance at her loafers. "If I were you, I'd put on sneakers for this trip."

"You're right—I guess," Nancy said with a faraway look.

"Is something bothering you?" Ned asked.

That was enough to make the girl detective

give a detailed account of what had just occurred. "I'm positive Angela was about to mention the name of some lake when we were cut off," Nancy said. "If only she weren't tied up at the theater now—"

"All we have to do is look at a large map of River Heights," Ned interrupted, following the girl into the house.

"I wish," Nancy said in an unhappy tone. "Do you have any idea how many lakes there are in this area?"

Ned shrugged. "A hundred?"

"No, not a hundred, but there are at least three or four big ones. It'll take days to scout each one."

"So?"

"So—we don't have that much time," Nancy went on. "Every day we spend searching for Phyllis Pruett will be one less spent helping Cliff find out who he is."

The girl's voice rippled a little, causing Ned to set his hands on her shoulders. "The important thing is that Cliff has a home now," he said gently.

Nancy lifted her face in a smile and sighed. "Guess I'm just a bit edgy these days."

Ned did not comment, but he sensed that Mr. Drew's trouble with the townspeople of River Heights was the source of Nancy's continuing distress. She hurried upstairs to change her shoes, pausing on the landing long enough to call down to Ned.

"How many lakes do you think we can cover by midnight?" She grinned.

"At least a dozen." Ned chuckled.

When Nancy returned, she was carrying a road map of River Heights.

"This has *everything* on it—even major landmarks like our new shopping mall on Oak Boulevard," Nancy said brightly.

"Does it also show Phyllis's retreat?" Ned teased, watching the map unfurl on the dining room table.

"That would be nice, wouldn't it?" Nancy remarked. She cast a glance at the two bodies of water indicated on either side of a mountain ridge near the River Heights Airport. A third one lay farther south near Castleton.

"They always say to try and kill two birds with one stone," Ned quipped.

"So we'll start with these two first," Nancy said, pointing to Swain Lake and Green Pond.

In less than an hour, the couple was following a steep road that led to the latter. At the top of the hill they found a lookout point where they stopped the car.

"There it is—Green Pond!" Nancy exclaimed as she gazed at a shimmer of greenish-blue water below that spread out fish-like behind an outcrop.

"See anything that looks like a retreat?" Ned asked.

"No, but there's a little bunch of stores at the bottom of this road," Nancy observed, "and people who visit the retreat do need supplies once in a while."

"Right on," Ned said as they leaped back into the car.

First stop was a delicatessen that offered an array of salads, cold cuts, and household items. The twosome were of only moderate interest to the few people standing in line at the counter. As soon as the customers left the store, Nancy spoke to the clerk, asking if he knew of any retreat in the area.

"Can't say that I do," he replied immediately, then pursed his lips. "But I have heard of something like that over on Swain Lake."

A surge of excitement pulsed through the girl. "Do you know where it is exactly?" Nancy asked.

"No, I don't, but you might take a ride over there. Someone's bound to be able to tell you."

"Thanks a lot!" the couple exclaimed, dashing outside.

"See, I told you we'd find it just like that," Ned said, snapping his fingers.

"It almost seems too easy," Nancy replied.

As they rode through the countryside, Nancy kept her eyes on the landscape, thinking that by chance she might glimpse a house or perhaps a hotel that had been converted into a retreat. All she saw, however, was an elderly man working in a garden carved out of the woodsy hillside.

"According to the map, Swain Lake should be no more than a few miles on the other side of the ridge," Ned remarked. Almost immediately, he spotted a road sign in the distance. "Maybe that's it."

He pressed down on the accelerator and within a few seconds reached the entrance to a motel lodge. Several cars were parked outside, and a young couple with two small children, an assortment of suitcases, and fishing gear emerged from one.

"Which way to the lake?" Nancy called out to the visitors.

"Down there," the man said, pointing to a trail behind the lodge.

Ned was eager to investigate, but Nancy suggested they inquire further.

"Who knows, maybe someone in the lodge can tell us exactly where the retreat is," Nancy said, "and save us a long walk."

"Not to mention a romantic hike through weeds," Ned concurred as he noticed a tangle of overgrowth along the trail.

The lodge was as rustic inside as it was outside. Gingham curtains hung on the windows, and there were straw rugs on the old floor that creaked under the visitors' feet as they approached the hotel desk. The young couple whom they had spoken to earlier had just finished registering, and the clerk glanced briefly at Nancy and Ned.

"May I help you?" he asked pleasantly, causing Nancy to explain the reason they were in the area.

When she finished speaking, her listener said, "I moved here only a little while ago. But let me ask one of the fellows in the back office. He may know about the retreat."

As he excused himself, the couple took advantage of the time to look at the handful of people seated around the lobby. All were dressed casually, with the exception of one man who was in a business suit. But as the desk clerk returned with a co-worker, the man disappeared upstairs.

"This is Mr. Keshav Lal," the clerk said by way of introduction. The man's mocha complexion, large, brown eyes, and name suggested to Nancy that he was probably from India.

"You are looking for Ramaswami?" Lal inquired.

"I don't know, am I?" Nancy said in surprise.

Her heart was thumping fast as she realized that she was on the brink of an important discovery!

"Yes, we are," Ned said, seizing the information instantly. "Where can we find Mr. Ramaswami?"

"We call him Swami," Lal corrected. He laughed quietly. "But I'm afraid that is all I can tell you."

"I don't understand," Nancy said, adding, "If you attend his retreat, you must—"

Before Nancy could finish the sentence,

however, the man in the business suit suddenly reappeared. He leaned over the counter, tapping his fingers in irritation.

"My calls have been disconnected at least twice," he complained to the desk clerk.

"I'm sorry, Mr. Flannery."

Flannery! That was the name of the woman whom Phyllis Pruett had been staying with. Were the two related?

For an instant, Nancy glanced at him. There was a familiarity about his face, but she couldn't place it.

"Excuse me," she said, addressing the man. "I'm looking for a girl by the name of Phyllis Pruett. I believe she's been living with people named Flannery—"

"Don't know her," he said abruptly, letting Mr. Lal resume his conversation with the girl.

"Give me your name first, please," he said.

"I'm Nancy Drew, and this is my friend, Ned Nickerson."

As Nancy spoke, Lal flashed his eyes away from her at someone else—Flannery, perhaps.

"Now will you tell us where the swami is?" she asked, pretending not to have noticed Lal's reaction to her.

"By all means. You will find a large cabin at the foot of these woods near the lake," the man said. "There is a trail—"

"I think we saw it," Ned interrupted.

"Well, it is a fairly long walk—almost a mile."

"In that case, we ought to get going," she told Ned, adding as they left, "Don't look back, but that guy Flannery is watching us."

"And don't look ahead either," Ned remarked, "'cause the sky's about to burst wide open."

"It's not going to rain!" Nancy said. "Come on, I'll race you to the lake!"

The couple darted toward the trail that had buried itself in an overgrowth of vines and almost disappeared entirely. Now and then they paused to glance down the slope of trees, waiting for a glimpse of the cabin retreat.

"I hope we're on the right track," Ned said as he felt a drizzle of water on his neck. "Because if we're not, we're in for a flood."

"Oh, Ned, it's only a light sprinkle," Nancy insisted, but, as the boy had predicted, in less than a minute rain began to pour.

It tore leaves and small branches off the trees, obscuring the trail and the hikers' vision. How much farther did they have to go?

"Let's turn back!" Ned shouted through the torrential rain.

Nancy, who was ahead of him, said something in reply, but Ned did not hear it. He hung back, ready to head for the lodge again and hoping Nancy would follow. She plunged deeper into the woods, however, glancing around only for a second.

The rainwater had seeped through Ned's clothes. "Where are you going?" Nancy cried out.

"Back to the motel," Ned said. "Come on!"

But the girl detective was determined to stay on the path to the lake. What difference did it make if she got wetter? She was already soaked to the skin.

Reluctantly, Ned yielded and trekked after her. The rain let up in spurts, and finally the couple reached a small clearing at the edge of the woods.

"That must be the place!" Nancy exclaimed when a cabin came into view.

She raced forward, feeling a chill in her bones, while Ned observed a woman peering through the window in the door. The light behind her suddenly went out and she pulled the shade down.

9

Cabin Captive

As Nancy and Ned leaped up the steps, Nancy dived for the cabin door, pounding on it with her fists.

"Hello-o," she cried, ignoring the drawn shade.

"If this is supposed to be a popular retreat," Ned said, "there sure doesn't seem to be much activity around here."

"Maybe everybody's meditating," Nancy suggested.

But as she spoke, the doorknob turned and opened, revealing the woman again.

"I don't want no more people staying here," she snapped.

Nancy told her that they were looking for Ramaswami.

"Who?" the woman asked.

"The swami," Ned repeated. "Do you know of him?"

"Not personally. But a bunch of people got turned away from his place because it was full up, so they came here."

"When was this?" Nancy inquired.

"Last weekend," the woman said. "They stayed here one night. Paid me, of course, but what a mess they left—dirty dishes everywhere."

"Where exactly is the swami's retreat?" Ned questioned.

"Stay on that trail," the woman replied, pointing to an opening in the woods behind the cabin. "You can't miss it, and when you see Mr. Swami, tell him I don't want any more visitors!"

She closed the door on Nancy and Ned. The rain had ended, leaving puddles of water in the softened earth which the couple now treaded across. The warming rays of the sun that began to emerge penetrated their wet clothes, making their clothing more tolerable as they walked in the woods.

"Are you with me?" Nancy said to Ned in a half-teasing voice.

"What do you think?" came the reply.

"Well, for a minute there I thought—" But Nancy did not have a chance to finish talking.

There was a scuffle of feet and the sound of branches breaking, which caused her to halt quickly.

In that split second before she could see what had happened to Ned, hands grabbed her waist and a scarf saturated with a strange honey-sweet fluid was stuffed in her mouth. She yanked her body forward, struggling to free herself, but the pungent odor soon overwhelmed her and Nancy fell limp against her attackers.

Meanwhile, Bess and George had finished their shopping excursion a bit earlier than they had anticipated.

"Why don't we pay a visit to Cliff?" Bess suggested to her cousin. "I'm sure he'd like to have some company."

George agreed, and after the girls dropped off their mothers at home, they headed for the Drew house. When they rang the doorbell, however, Hannah did not answer it.

"That's odd," George commented.

"Maybe Hannah went shopping, too," Bess replied.

"Even so, I'm surprised Cliff doesn't hear the bell," George said. "Of course, he could be sleeping."

As the girls headed for the driveway again, they saw Hannah Gruen coming up the walk with a shopping cart filled with groceries.

"I told you so." Bess giggled and called out to the housekeeper. "We just stopped by to see Cliff."

"Oh, and having done so, you're leaving now, before I've even had a chance to give you a piece of cake," Hannah said, halting the cart.

"On the contrary," Bess replied. "We haven't seen Cliff at all. We rang the bell, but he didn't answer it."

The housekeeper appeared perplexed. "He must still be sleeping."

Everyone stepped inside the hallway. Hannah set her packages down in the kitchen, then went upstairs. Cliff's room was empty!

"Cliff?" she called out.

There was no response.

"Will you girls check downstairs for him,

while I look around up here?" Hannah asked Bess and George.

They darted from room to room, glancing through windows to see if perhaps he had gone outside. They panicked as they realized that the young amnesia victim had disappeared!

"This is terrible, terrible!" Hannah cried. "I wasn't out of this house more than an hour. Oh, what if something has happened to him? It's all my fault!"

The girls tried to comfort the woman, wishing that Nancy were there and wondering what to do next.

"Let's call the police," Bess declared nervously.

"Good idea," George said, dashing to the hall telephone. But she picked it up and put it down instantly. "We shouldn't jump to conclusions," she said. "After all, there's no sign of a break-in anywhere, and Hannah, you locked all the doors before you left, didn't you?"

"Yes—oh, certainly."

"Well, then, it seems to me that Cliff may have simply decided to go for a walk."

Somehow, though, that did not seem likely to Bess.

"I suggest we wait a little while before calling the police," George went on.

"But what if you're wrong?" Bess replied anxiously.

"If I'm wrong, then I'm wrong."

"That's the craziest logic I ever heard," Bess said, racing to the telephone.

"Okay, suit yourself," George said, stepping away from her cousin. "But you're going to feel really foolish when Cliff walks in the door."

Hannah, in the meantime, had paid little attention to the banter between the girls. She sat frozen in her chair, hearing Nancy's earlier request repeat itself in her mind.

"No matter what," the girl detective had told the housekeeper, "please don't leave Cliff alone while I'm gone today."

But the refrigerator needed replenishment and Hannah had attended to the errand as quickly as she could, when she was unable to persuade the local store to make a delivery.

"The police are coming over right away," Bess said now, drawing Hannah out of her stupor.

"Thank goodness," she answered vaguely. "Someone must find Cliff before Nancy comes home."

The young detective, however, lay bound on the damp floor of a cabin, near an old iron stove. The odor of mildew that cloyed the air had replaced that of the insidious drug, and Nancy's eyes flickered open.

She was at once aware of the sweet, antiseptic taste in her mouth and the fact that the scarf had been removed. She lifted her head, then let it sink back as a dull ache thudded through her skull.

Where am I? And where's Ned? she wondered dizzily.

The log ceiling dripped water now, sprinkling Nancy's face unevenly and causing her to slide out from under the leak. As she moved, she noticed something dark and slippery crawling over a crack in the floor. It was moving slowly, steadily toward her. A water snake!

Completely helpless, she shrieked in horror, but the sound caught in her throat and she continued to drag herself away from the creature.

"Oh!" Nancy cried as the viper raised its head, poised for a venomous strike.

Instantly, the girl swung her knees up, catching the rubber soles of her sneakers in a loose floorboard. To her amazement, it popped up and made the crack split wider. The snake plunged forward, tumbling into the pit of earth below.

Despite her relief, Nancy shivered, gazing through a rain-spattered window overhead. The sky was dark now, and even if she could loosen the rope around her wrists and ankles, she wondered if she could escape.

Her log prison was surrounded by tall trees, and without the benefit of the sun, she had no idea where she was nor how she could find her way to Swain Lake Lodge.

The other, more troubling thought was, What had happened to her friend, Ned Nickerson? Where had their abductors taken him?

I have to find Ned! I must! Nancy thought with determination.

10

Ned's Rescue

At the same time, Bess and George were talking with a young policeman in the Drew living room. Although the River Heights Police Department had a description of Cliff on file, the officer requested additional information.

"Since the young man has been staying here," the officer said, "has he undergone any physical changes?"

"Hardly," Hannah remarked from a corner chair. "He came here only today."

"Oh, I see," the policeman said, clearing his throat. "Well, did he say anything at all that might give a clue to where he went? Judging merely from the looks of things, I'd say he might have left voluntarily."

George flashed an I-told-you-so glance at her cousin.

"Do you suppose he could have gone back to the hospital for some reason?" Bess suggested.

"Now why would he do that?" George muttered.

As she spoke, the policeman was examining a spot on the carpet which the others had overlooked near the entranceway.

"Chloroform," he said crisply.

His listeners gasped. "Then Cliff was kidnapped!" Bess exclaimed.

"But the front door was locked when we got here," George pointed out.

"Maybe Cliff recognized the person and let him in," Hannah put in.

"Or maybe—" the policeman said, heading for the back door. Bess and the others trailed after him. "Just as I thought," the young officer concluded. He pointed to a hole in the kitchen screen door.

The cousins now stepped outside, pinning their eyes to the ground for footprints.

"There! Look there!" George cried as prints loomed from the driveway. They traveled across the dampened grass to the back steps.

"He must've been very tall," Bess said, observing the long stride and large footprints.

While the mystery of Cliff's disappearance had not been resolved, Nancy, too, was seeking an answer to freedom. She twisted her arms, causing the rope to cut into her wrists, but steeled herself against the pain, looking for something, anything with which to sever the rope.

There! she gasped, spotting a thick nail that protruded from the base of the wall. It wasn't much, but it might work!

The young captive pulled close, hooking the rope over the iron head. Back and forth she rubbed the twine, hoping to wear down the strong threads, but they held firm.

I'll never get out of here! Nancy moaned.

Her arms ached now, and she lay back against the wall, intending to relax only for a minute, but instead falling fast asleep. When she awoke, two birds were chirping on the window ledge above and the sky had begun to lighten.

Morning had come, and Nancy had lost precious time in her search for Ned. Although the hours of rest had given her renewed energy, her body felt stiff and she longed for freedom even more.

Again she worked on the rope, stopping only when she heard the sound of footsteps outside the cabin.

Was it her captor? the girl wondered.

Panic-stricken, she froze and quietly lifted the rope off the nail.

Who is it? she thought anxiously as the door creaked open, revealing muddy sneakers and blue jeans.

"Ned!" she cried happily.

"Nancy, are you all right?" he asked immediately.

As Nancy spouted several questions, Ned began cutting the rope at her feet with a penknife. The rope binding Nancy's wrists did not sever so easily, but after several minutes of steady pressure, it, too, came free.

"Your wrists—" Ned murmured when he saw the deep red bruises.

"I'm fine," Nancy insisted, even though she felt a twinge of pain. "Really I am, Ned."

But the boy suspected otherwise.

"Forget me. Tell me what happened to you," the girl went on. She got to her feet slowly, with Ned's help.

"They dumped me in another shelter a few yards from here," he said, adding, "I still have a throbbing headache from the chloroform."

"They must've given you an extra dose," Nancy commented. "I didn't see who the men were. Did you?"

"Nope, and so far as I know they never came to check on me."

Nancy paused momentarily as they stepped outside into the sunlight. "I just don't get it—why us?" she said.

"Maybe someone doesn't want us to find the retreat," Ned suggested, a thought that had occurred to Nancy as well.

"But why?" she repeated. "Retreats are places for quiet and meditation, not for trouble."

Nancy linked her arm into Ned's, leaning on him until the stiffness in her legs had passed. Although she would have liked to continue the hunt for the swami's retreat, she knew that she must get home quickly. The Drew household would have realized Nancy had not come home and they would be frantic.

"How far do you think we are from the lodge?" the girl asked Ned.

"I have no idea, but my guess is that we're at least a mile away."

The thought of the long trudge back through

the same tangled woods made Nancy groan. But as the sun's warmth enveloped her again, she smiled.

"At least we don't have to swim through another flood," she remarked, letting Ned lead the way when the trail narrowed to a thin footpath.

By the time they reached the lodge, they realized that they had returned along a different route. But where it lay in relation to the one they had taken the day before remained a mystery.

"I wonder if there's a road to the retreat," the young detective said as they headed for the car. "Maybe I ought to ask Mr. Lal." And without giving Ned a chance to reply, she raced into the building.

There were different clerks on duty, however, and when she asked for the Indian man, she was informed that he was not in and wouldn't be back for a few days.

Nancy returned to the car, reporting the little she had learned.

"Don't worry," Ned said. "We'll track that retreat down eventually."

"I hope so," Nancy replied. She lapsed into

silence, saying no more on the subject until they were inside the Drew home. Then, before Hannah or Mr. Drew could reveal their news, the couple spilled out their story in detail.

"By the way, where's Cliff?" Nancy inquired when she finished speaking.

"Oh, Nancy, please don't blame me," Hannah pleaded, causing the girl's face to close in fear.

"Has something happened to him?" she asked.

"We don't know," Mr. Drew replied.

"He's been kidnapped!" Hannah blurted out. "Someone came in while I went food shopping and took him!"

The woman fixed her eyes steadily on the girl. "Bess and George were here, too, when we found out he was missing. We called the police right away."

As the reality of what had occurred sank in, Nancy sat down next to her father. "This is awful," she said. "I should never have left the house."

"Nothing else was taken," Hannah remarked.

"Only Cliff," Nancy murmured dejectedly.

The housekeeper bit her lips as a rim of tears

developed in her eyes. "Excuse me, everybody," she said, and left the room.

"Maybe I should go too," Ned said. "I'll call you later, Nancy."

The girl stared at her father for some offer of advice. "I don't know what to suggest, dear," he said. "I'm sure the police will find Cliff."

"But he was our responsibility, Dad," Nancy answered.

She telephoned Bess and George, and after they agreed to meet her for lunch at a downtown restaurant, Nancy decided to talk with the Drews' neighbors.

To her delight, she learned that the son of one couple had noticed a car speeding away from the Drew home the previous afternoon.

"Cool car," the boy said. "Stripes and everything."

"Did you notice the license plate?" Nancy asked excitedly.

"I noticed *everything*," he said, repeating the number. "197-MAP."

By now, Nancy's heart was pounding as she wondered if the vehicle was the one she had seen at Rosemont Hospital and the one that might have caused Tommy Johnson's accident!

She raced back to her house and telephoned the information to the police, who promptly fed it into a computer. It was only a matter of minutes before the girl had an answer.

"We have traced the owner of the car," the officer reported. "His name is Dev Singh. He lives near the river."

Nancy quickly jotted down the address, eager to reveal the discovery to her friends.

What intrigued her most, however, was the man's name. Was he from India? If so, might he be the man who had accompanied the bearded stranger to Mr. Jhaveri's shop?

11

Cancellation!

While Nancy stared at the unusual name she had written on a notepad, she also noticed a bright yellow flier poking through the morning mail on the hall table. It was an announcement from the River Heights Music Festival, which she opened quickly.

"Canceled?" she said, mystified, as her eyes fell on the large stamp mark that obliterated the names of several artist groups, including the Jansen Theater Troupe, which was scheduled to perform that evening.

I wonder if Dad knows about this, the girl detective thought.

Carson Drew, however, had already left for a business appointment, and the only way she could get some answers was to go to the River

Heights Theater herself. Taking a quick glance at her watch, she pocketed the flier and dashed to her car.

It was no surprise to Nancy when she arrived that at least thirty ticket holders to the festival had begun to descend on the box office. Many of them were carrying the cancellation notice and complaining angrily.

"Excuse me," the girl found herself saying over and over as she weaved through the crowd now queuing up into long lines.

"Hey, kid," one man snarled at Nancy when she stepped in front of him. "Where do you think you're going? I was here first."

"I only want to find out where the manager is," Nancy insisted.

"Don't we all," he replied, as a tall, angular man strode into view.

"Ladies and gentlemen, I am Mr. Hillyer, the manager," he said, "and I want you to know that none of the performances have been canceled. The notice is a mistake—"

"I'll say it was!" one irritated woman cut in loudly, causing the people around her to echo the complaint.

"Please—please. Let me explain," the manager replied. He raised his hand, signaling the crowd to be quiet. "Your tickets will be honored at every performance. Nothing has been canceled. Believe me."

Somebody must've gotten hold of the festival's mailing list and sent that announcement just to stir up trouble, Nancy concluded.

She waited for the crowd to disperse, then approached the manager.

"I'm Carson Drew's daughter," she said brightly, watching the man's relaxed demeanor fade.

Had the ill will of some of the townspeople toward the attorney filtered down to the festival management?

"What can I do for you?" the manager answered coolly.

"Well, I was wondering if you had any idea about the person who sent that cancellation notice."

"Why don't you ask your father?" the man snapped, and before Nancy could come to her father's defense, he excused himself.

Now, more than ever, she was determined to vindicate the Drew name.

All the way to the restaurant where she was to meet George and Bess, the girl constructed her next move. When they were all finally seated at a vacant table, Bess's eyes sparkled.

"You're awfully happy today," Nancy commented.

Bess shook her head excitedly, while George smiled pleasantly. Had the cousins made some important discovery? Nancy wondered.

"Don't keep me in suspense," she told them. "Did you find Cliff, or do you know where—"

"No, nothing that spectacular," George mumbled.

"But I think we've figured out an ingenious way to find his ring," Bess put in. "Since it's so unusual—"

"And valuable," George added.

"All we have to do is put an ad in the newspaper," her cousin finished.

"But if the guy who ran off with it is a thief, why would he even consider selling it back? I'm sure he's not stupid."

"True, but I bet he's greedy," Bess replied, "and if the reward is tempting enough, he might just fall into the trap."

Nancy half agreed, but was far from convinced and changed the subject momentarily. She brought the girls up to date on everything that had happened so far, ending with the information about Dev Singh.

"Do you have time now to check out his address?" Nancy asked her friends.

"Sure," George said. "Let's go."

The threesome ate their lunch quickly, then headed for Nancy's car, as another idea occurred to Bess.

"Mr. Jhaveri's store isn't far from here," she noted. "I'd like to find out what he thinks Cliff's ring is worth."

So the girls changed direction and walked a few blocks up the street. There were only four customers inside the store, and when they dwindled to one lone woman admiring the contents of a display case in the corner, Nancy and the girls spoke to the jeweler.

"How much would you estimate the ring we showed you is worth?" Nancy asked.

"Oh, that's hard to say. The gold itself could bring a handsome price."

"Can't you be more specific?" Bess pressed him.

"Offhand, I'm afraid not. But if you give me a little time to think, I may be able to give you an answer."

As he talked, Nancy thought she detected someone in the office behind the man. But then she realized it was only an unframed photograph that reflected in a wall mirror. She had not paid attention to it on previous visits. This time, however, she found herself transfixed. It was a picture of someone who bore an uncanny resemblance to Keshav Lal!

"Is something wrong?" George whispered to the girl.

"N-no," Nancy said, blinking her eyes in another direction. Then, on impulse, she asked Mr. Jhaveri if he knew Lal.

"He's my cousin," the man remarked with a touch of surprise in his voice. "You know him?"

"I met him at the Swain Lake Lodge," Nancy said, stringing out her thoughts slowly. "It just hit me that you might have some information about the swami's retreat."

Mr. Jhaveri shook his head vigorously. "I've never been there," he said.

"But you are aware of it," Nancy said.

"Yes, of course. Many of us Indians are, but I personally am not a follower of Ramaswami."

Nancy was even tempted to inquire if he knew someone by the name of Dev Singh, but decided not to until she had investigated him further. Instead, she continued her current line of questioning.

"Mr. Lal directed me to a trail," Nancy said, "but I'd bet there's another, easier route."

The man simply shrugged his shoulders, and as the lady customer came forward, he took advantage of the opportunity to escape from the girls.

They left, puzzling over their latest discovery.

"He seemed awfully nervous when you mentioned Lal's name," George told Nancy.

"I know, but why?"

No answer occurred to any of them as they drove to the address which the police said belonged to Dev Singh. When the young detectives reached it, however, they were completely stumped, because standing on the site was not a house or an apartment building, but a place called Hamburger Haven!

"Too bad we already ate lunch," George said, as their car hummed in the driveway.

"And too bad we're not getting anywhere," Bess added with a sigh.

Nancy, too, had secretly begun to feel defeated, but she flashed an optimistic smile at her friends. "I have a hunch there's an answer to this mystery just around the corner!" she exclaimed.

12

Escape Lane

"What makes you so optimistic?" Bess asked Nancy as she backed the car out of the driveway.

"Because I just realized we're on the wrong street." The girl laughed. "Singh's place is on River Lane, not River Drive."

She pointed to the bold green sign that hung a quarter of a mile down the road. There was an exit off the drive for River Lane.

The ride along the water's edge was exhilarating as the girls rolled down the car windows and let the breeze carry in the fresh, sweet smell of grass and wildflowers.

"Wouldn't it be nice to have a picnic down here?" George suggested.

"Why, I can't believe you said that, George Fayne," her cousin teased. "You, a girl who never thinks about food."

"It's a great idea," Nancy interposed, believing they'd all be ready for a celebration when the latest mysteries were solved.

The question was, Would they ever be?

She turned off the drive, jogging onto one street, then another, until she was on River Lane. It curved into the countryside, no houses immediately visible behind fences of hedge and poplar trees. Then, with no forewarning, the road stopped.

"Now what?" Bess said, as Nancy halted the car.

"This is getting to be ridiculous," she remarked unhappily and swung the car around. "I didn't see one house number, did you?"

"Uh-uh," George said.

"Me neither," Bess added, but on the return ride Nancy slowed the car down considerably, pausing at a trail of gravel off the road. "Driveway?" Bess said.

"We'll soon find out," Nancy said, making the sharp turn.

The car dipped into several potholes, which caused Nancy to keep her eyes trained for others and not on the house at the top of the hillock. When they pulled in front of it at last, they all sighed, feeling the ride itself had been an accomplishment.

"It doesn't look like anyone's around," Nancy commented shortly.

"There's no house number, either," Bess said, suddenly feeling queasy. "I don't know if this is such a hot idea, Nancy. I mean, what if Singh does live here and he tries to kidnap us too."

"For one thing, there are three of us and only one of him," George declared.

"How do you know?" her cousin replied.

Undaunted, however, Nancy went boldly up the front steps to ring the doorbell. No one came immediately, and she stood on her toes to glance through the small windowpane at the top of the door.

"This must be Singh's place," she told the others as she stared at a pair of batik wall hangings with Indian motifs.

"Oh, let's get out of here," Bess pleaded, but her listeners did not pay attention.

Nancy cupped her ear against the door, sensing for a moment that she had heard noises from within. Had Singh brought Cliff there?

Had the young man heard the car approaching, and was he struggling to let the visitors know of his imprisonment?

The girl detective was determined to find out!

"We can't just break in," Bess warned, while Nancy skirted the house to a side window, trying to open it.

"But what if Cliff is tied up in there?" Nancy countered.

"Even so, I vote we bring the police back with a search warrant," Bess said.

But as she spoke, they could hear the purr of a car engine at the bottom of the driveway.

"Oh, somebody's coming!" Bess exclaimed nervously. "What'll we do?"

"They'll see us for sure," George said, glancing at Nancy's car.

"C'mon!" Nancy declared, leaping toward it. "Those potholes will slow them down a little bit."

She turned the ignition and pressed the accelerator gently, letting the car roll forward onto a crescent of grass that curved around the far side of the house.

"It's the best I can do for now," the young detective said. She switched off the engine and listened to the sound of the other one growing louder. "You wait here," she told her friends. "I want to see who it is."

"But Nan—" Bess cried fearfully.

Her friend nonetheless stepped out of her car, leaving the door open in case she wanted to dive back in fast, and ran to the high bushes that hugged the front wall. She peered through the thick cover of leaves, listening to two men. They sat talking and, to her relief, did not seem to notice the wheel marks of the car that lay ahead. Their car, she observed quickly, did not match the description of the one her neighbor's son had seen at the Drew home.

Who are they? Nancy wondered as the driver finally appeared. Then, almost instantaneously, his companion slid out into view.

It's the man in the business suit I saw at Swain Lake Lodge! Nancy gasped, suddenly realizing that he and the bearded stranger who had attacked Cliff in the hospital were one and the same! With him was the tall Indian man who had been with him in Mr. Jhaveri's store!

We have to get the police! the girl said to herself.

She darted to the car, telling her friends everything as the men went inside the house.

"But we're stuck!" Bess cried. "And as soon as they realize we're here, we'll be done for, too!"

Nancy, however, had studied the slope of lawn that sprawled alongside the driveway that now held an obstacle—the men's car!

"Hang on!" she said, starting the ignition again, and spun the vehicle across the gravel and down the grassy incline, bypassing the potholes and lurching onto the road.

Bess had closed her eyes in a shiver of fear as Nancy urged the gas pedal.

"There's a public phone on River Drive," George remarked, seeing the glass booth come into view.

Without saying a word, Nancy screeched the car to a halt and leaped out, dialing River Heights police. She told them where she was and where she suspected Cliff was being held captive, then returned to her friends.

"They're on their way," Nancy said, "and they advised me to stay here."

"Thank goodness," Bess replied, still trembling as a patrol car with two officers inside whizzed toward them.

In the driver's seat was the young officer who had gone to the Drews' home when Cliff was reported missing. He signaled Nancy to follow.

When they turned onto River Lane, Nancy flashed her headlights, indicating the gravel driveway several yards ahead. The patrol car slowed down, pitching over the potholes with caution and coming to a halt when they reached the car parked in front of the house. Nancy and the girls pulled in behind them, hurrying after the officers.

"Open up!" the young policeman yelled, knocking hard on the door.

To Nancy's amazement, someone responded immediately. It was the Indian man whom she had seen arrive only moments before.

"Are you Dev Singh?" she asked at once.

"Why no, and I never heard of him." His high cheekbones resolved into deep-set eyes that gaped at Nancy in puzzlement.

"Let me see your identification," the policeman said, prompting the man to pull out an immigration card that bore the name Prem Nath.

"I've been in this country only a short time, so I don't have any credit cards." He chuckled softly.

The other policeman, meantime, flashed a search warrant, saying, "We're looking for a young man who was kidnapped recently."

"And you think I am responsible?" the Indian replied, laughing.

"Where is the man you came with?" George asked.

"What man?"

"His name is Flannery," Nancy said crisply, even though she suspected that it was an alias.

"I don't know what you are talking about. Now please—"

But the officers moved past him, the girls also, and they spread out to look in every room. Flannery was not there, and neither was Cliff! Had Flannery ducked out of the house to hide among the trees? Nancy was tempted to search the grounds, until the police spoke apologetically to the man.

"We're sorry to have troubled you, Mr. Nath," one of the men said, satisfied that he had committed no wrongdoing.

Nancy, however, remained unconvinced. She knew Flannery, or whoever the man was, had taken Cliff's ring. Unfortunately, though, he had escaped capture this time. It was useless to pursue the subject with the police until she had more definite evidence.

"I just don't get it," George said. "The car was registered in Singh's name at this address,

111

but there's a guy named Nath living here."

"Doesn't matter," Bess said. "According to Nancy's neighbor, he saw Singh's car leave the Drew home, but he didn't say Cliff was in it. We assume so, but there's nothing conclusive to prove it."

"Maybe Singh did live at the house at one time, but moved out before his car registration came due for renewal," Nancy added. "Anyway, as you say, Bess, none of this matters a whole lot. We just want to find Cliff."

As she drove toward home, she began to think about Swain Lake Lodge again. What was Flannery doing up there?

13

Technical Attack

By the time the girls reached the parking lot where Bess and George had left their car, they asked Nancy about her plans for the rest of the day.

"As a matter of fact," she said, "I haven't any—"

"I don't believe it," Bess said.

"Other than visiting Tommy, calling Angela Pruett, hunting for Phyllis, and—"

"St-o-p!" George teased, putting her hands over her ears. "Don't you ever take a break?"

"Oh, sure." Nancy laughed. "I was just going to ask if you'd like to see *Oklahoma* tonight? The Jansen Theater Troupe is putting it on."

"I'd love to," Bess said happily, "and maybe Dave would."

"How about the six of us going together?" George put in.

Nancy nodded in agreement, asking the cousins to check with their friends Dave Evans and Burt Eddleton while she called Ned.

"Can you make reservations, too?" she asked the girls.

"No problem," Bess said. "Talk to you later."

"'Bye," Nancy replied, heading her car for Rosemont Hospital and a quick visit with Tommy Johnson.

To her amazement and delight, she found him walking in a leg cast with the aid of crutches.

"You'll be out of here in no time," she said to the little boy.

"I hope so," he declared, smiling. "There's nobody to play with around here."

He lay the crutches against his bed, allowing Nancy to help him up.

"Well, what about me?" she asked, pretending to pout.

"You're different, Nancy," he said. "Everybody else just wants to take my temperature."

The girl laughed, opening a small shopping

bag and peering inside with great relish.

"What's in there?" Tommy said eagerly.

Nancy strung out the surprise until she thought the boy would jump out of bed. "Here you are," the girl said, producing a toy racing car.

"Zowie!" Tommy cried happily. He ran the tiny wheels up and down his cast, then over the mattress, onto the night table, and back again.

Nancy giggled. "I'm sure your doctor never dreamed that cast would turn into a racetrack!"

When she left the boy's room, he was still playing with the car, rumbling like an engine, and laughing in between.

"I'll be back," the girl told him, though she wasn't sure when her next visit would be.

She stopped by the nurses' station to leave a message for Lisa Scotti, and was pleased to find her friend there in person.

"The strangest thing happened this morning," Lisa whispered to Nancy. "We got a phone call from someone who said his name was Cliff."

"You're kidding!" Nancy replied.

"Of course, I was positive it was some crackpot," Lisa went on.

"Why do you say that?"

"Because I knew Cliff was staying at your house."

"Not anymore," Nancy said, revealing the full story.

Lisa was completely shocked, saying she wouldn't have bothered to tell Nancy about the call except that she had stopped by the hospital.

"Oh, Lisa, you must tell me everything that happens if it's pertinent to Cliff's case."

"Now that I think about it," Lisa said, "the voice did sound like Cliff's, but I can't be certain. There was a lot of static in the background."

"What did he say?" Nancy questioned.

"Not much, really, but it had something to do with singing."

"Singing or the name Singh?"

Lisa shrugged. "As I said, the voice wasn't too clear."

If only the young nurse had known about the disappearance, Nancy thought, she might have tried to trace the phone call.

Thinking of missed opportunities, Nancy decided to try contacting Angela Pruett again. The telephone seemed to be working, but the harpist was not home—all the more reason, Nancy mused, why she should attend the performance at the River Heights Theater that night.

Nancy spoke briefly to Ned, who had already heard from the other Emerson boys, and despite a minor problem that had to do with the availability of a car for the evening, everyone had decided to meet at the Drew home.

The sky had thickened with clouds and there was the promise of another rainstorm.

"Don't forget your umbrella, dear," Hannah advised Nancy as the group left, but Ned waved his, a large, black one that could amply cover two people.

When they arrived at the theater, Nancy was struck by the small, scattered audience.

"Where is everybody?" Burt asked.

"Maybe they were afraid to come out in a storm," George said.

"But it isn't even raining yet," her cousin stated.

Nancy, however, surmised that a number of ticket holders had received the cancellation notice and for whatever reasons had not yet called the theater for a refund. If they had, they would have been told the announcement was a hoax!

She thought no more about it, though, as the orchestra filed into the pit. She looked for

Angela, but someone else—another woman—was seated at the harp.

"Where is she?" Ned whispered to Nancy.

"I don't know."

But as the overture swelled, the young detective temporarily pushed her concern to the back of her mind. The medley of tunes was a welcome respite from earlier events of the day, soaring to a climax and dissolving when the curtain opened.

The stage, however, remained pitch-black for several minutes as the first actors entered. Then harsh red lights came on.

"What's going on?" Bess said.

That was what everyone wanted to know. The actors moved mechanically through the scene, saying their lines and singing with as much ease as they could muster. But the red lights turned blue, then amber, and the din of the audience competed against the sound on stage, causing the lead singer to stop in the middle of his number.

"Ladies and gentlemen," he said, as the overhead lights went out abruptly. "House lights, please," he instructed someone offstage.

Nancy slid out of her seat and hurried to the

back of the theater, without waiting to hear the announcement.

"I'm coming with you," Ned whispered.

"No, stay here," Nancy said. "I'll be back in a second."

She darted through the lobby doors, spying another one marked EMPLOYEES ONLY. Did it lead to the sound booth where the technician controlled the sound and lighting systems?

Nancy turned the knob, ready to climb the inside stairway, when a young man bolted out the door. He was no more than twenty and had shoulder-length brown hair that blew off his neck as he ran down the front steps.

"Stop!" Nancy cried. She dashed after him, but her high dress heels slowed her down.

The boy had jumped in a car and roared away in the darkness before she could catch him. Instantly, she hurried back into the theater, racing to the employees' door and up the steps.

"Oh!" she gasped upon seeing a man slumped forward over a board of dials.

Next to him lay a wooden rod that had obviously been used to knock him out!

"What's going on here?" a voice barked behind her. It was the festival manager. Nancy turned sharply, giving him full view of the injured man. "Are you responsible for this, Miss Drew?"

"Me?" Nancy said, aghast. She felt her former irritation, but kept her temper in check and quickly explained what had happened. "He needs a doctor. Excuse me while I find one."

The stream of people prevented Nancy from getting an usher's attention, but as her friends appeared, she made her way toward them.

"Someone attacked the man in the sound and lighting booth," Nancy advised them. "We have to get a doctor for him."

"Is he bleeding?" George asked.

"No, but he's out cold."

Ned raced away from the group, negotiating through the slow-moving crowd to a man in a theater uniform at the far end of the lobby. Briefly, Ned reported the situation and the two of them hurried to a telephone in a rear office.

By the time they emerged again, Nancy had gone back to the booth, leaving the others to wait for Ned and the emergency squad.

The technician moaned quietly. His fingers curled over a switch, then spread out as he tried to lift his head.

"He'll be all right," the festival manager said.

He glared at Nancy. "Trouble seems to abound when you and your father are in our midst," he said sarcastically.

The young detective gulped, ignoring the comment. Instead, she leaned close to the technician.

"Please try not to move too much," she said gently. "You could have a concussion."

The man blinked his eyes slowly, murmuring, "I'm okay. That kid only tapped me."

But the eyes closed again, and the fingers stopped moving.

Ned, in the meantime, appeared in the doorway. "Rosemont is sending an ambulance right away," he said.

"That's good," Nancy said, noting the lump that had swelled through the victim's thinning hairline.

"There is no need for you to stick around," the manager told the couple. "I will take care of Vince from here on."

Nancy, however, did not wish to leave the theater until the ambulance arrived, so she and Ned returned to the lobby. The two large, glass doors were open now, and an approaching siren soon stopped as the hospital vehicle pulled in front.

"What was the announcement I missed?" Nancy asked her friends as two men in white uniforms wheeled in a stretcher.

"The star apologized for the interruption," Bess said, "but said they couldn't go on under such circumstances."

Burt revealed a handful of money. "Everybody got a refund on their tickets," he said.

"I wonder why they didn't offer to honor them for another evening," Nancy said.

"Well," George replied, "I did overhear one woman say to another that she doubted that she would want to come to such a poorly run operation again."

"What's on tomorrow night?" Dave inquired.

"Nancy has the schedule," Bess said.

"Whatever it is," Nancy put in, "I have a strong hunch that unless they strengthen security around here, the program could fall apart like this one did."

Now the group watched the ambulance team carry Vince through the employees' door. His head did not move as he lay on the stretcher.

How long would it be, Nancy wondered, before he could tell her about the incident? Had Vince expected the visitor, or was it a surprise attack?

14

Flannery Foolery

While the group followed the stretcher out, the festival manager hurried briskly toward his office.

"Boy, he's unfriendly," Bess said as they stepped out under the dark sky.

He was more than unfriendly, Nancy thought. He was downright antagonistic.

Since the performance had been cut short, the young people decided to stop somewhere for a light snack, giving them a chance to discuss a plan of action.

"Come to think of it," Nancy said, "I've yet to meet Dr. DeNiro."

"Young or old?" Ned asked.

"Young," Bess smirked, causing a mock frown to form on her listener's face.

"And rather nice-looking," George said.

"I thought you said you wanted to go to the Flannery house," Ned said to Nancy.

"Oh, that too."

"Well, I'm free tomorrow, if you want company," the young man offered.

"I could use an extra pair of eyes," Nancy teased.

"How about my sunglasses, then?" George said in a laughing voice.

"I'd rather take Ned, thank you," Nancy grinned.

As the conversation faded into light banter, the group temporarily forgot about the latest developments in the mysteries. When Nancy's telephone rang early the next morning, however, she was surprised and happy to hear Angela Pruett's voice.

"I've been so concerned about you!" Nancy told the harpist.

"I'm sorry. I should have called you sooner," Angela said, wavering as she went on. "But I received a short message from Phyllis."

"Yesterday?" Nancy interrupted.

"Yes, and she said she wanted to meet me at

Swain Lake Lodge in the afternoon."

Nancy listened intently as Angela explained how she had waited almost two hours for her sister to arrive, but she never did.

"I finally inquired at the desk," Angela said. "That's when I discovered a second message from Phyllis. All she said was that she couldn't come after all."

"Were both messages handwritten?" Nancy questioned.

"No. The first one was, but it was scribbled. The second one was phoned in by a woman, the clerk said."

"But not necessarily by Phyllis," Nancy remarked in a suspicious tone.

She immediately revealed her own experience at the same lodge, which now more than ever seemed integral to the mysteries she sought to solve. She described Lal and asked if Angela had seen him.

"No, I haven't," the harpist replied, pausing. "Now I'm wondering if I should go back to the lodge today. Phyllis said she might be able to come."

Somehow, the idea did not sit well with Nancy.

"The whole business seems very odd to me,

and I have a feeling you'll just find a third message," she sighed. "Anyway, don't you have a performance tonight?"

"I'm not sure," Angela said. "There's been some talk of canceling the rest of the week."

She had not yet heard about the catastrophe the night before, so Nancy gave her the details.

"Then I'm sure everything will be postponed," Angela said. "The festival has really turned into a fiasco, and what worries me most is that I may be out of a job sooner than I anticipated. I'd have to go home, and I can't. I just can't."

"We'll find Phyllis before that happens," Nancy assured her. "As a matter of fact, I'd like to see Mrs. Flannery. Do you have the address handy?"

Nancy refrained from telling the woman about the man identified as Flannery, whom she had seen at the lodge and later realized was the person who had attacked Cliff. There was no point in further upsetting Angela, Nancy decided.

So when the harpist gave her the information, the young detective merely thanked her and said she would be in touch. Ned was to arrive within the hour, so Nancy hurried to get ready.

When the doorbell rang, she greeted the young man in a new summer skirt and puff-sleeved blouse that complemented her lightly tanned complexion.

"Hi!" Ned smiled. "I gather we're not going on a hike in the woods today."

"Not in these I'm not," Nancy chuckled, taking a glance at the bare, white sandals she wore. "I'd probably wind up with a terrific case of poison ivy!"

"And who wants itchy feet when you're chasing down kidnappers!" Ned said, leading the way to the car.

They found the Flannery house without too much difficulty, and to their delight, Mrs. Flannery was there. She was at least twelve or fifteen years older than her visitors, a judgment they drew based on the line of her face. Her figure, on the other hand, was taut like an athlete's, and she exuded energy as she spoke.

"Yes?" she said crisply when she opened the door.

Nancy and Ned introduced themselves and said they were looking for Phyllis Pruett.

"She hasn't been here for a week," the woman said. "I haven't the vaguest idea where she went, and—"

"Did you call the police about her disappearance?"

"Who said anything about a disappearance?" Mrs. Flannery charged back. "She's only been gone a few days. I don't keep tabs on her, anyway. She pays me rent, and she comes and goes as she likes."

She started to close the door, but Nancy moved forward.

"May we come in for a minute?" she asked sweetly.

"Look, I have a lot of errands to do."

"It will only take a moment," Ned added, knowing that Nancy was hoping to pick up some clue to the whereabouts of the missing girl.

"I'd like to see her room, if you don't mind," Nancy said.

The woman rolled her tongue over her lips, then drew in air, hesitating to reply.

"You have no objection, do you?" the girl detective continued.

"No, why should I? Except maybe I don't know if Phyllis would appreciate letting strangers into her room."

"We're not really strangers," Nancy said quickly. "I'm a personal friend of Phyllis's sister, Angela, and she knows I'm here."

"Oh, uh-huh."

Still, the woman hung on the door, allowing less than foot space for anyone to enter. It was true that someone else might have reacted similarly to the girl's request, but Mrs. Flannery seemed unusually reluctant. Nancy would have inquired about the man whose name was the same as hers, except that she thought it unwise to reveal too much now.

Mrs. Flannery pulled the door back at last.

"Okay, come in," she said, "but you can't stay long."

She led the couple up a stairway and into a corridor that connected to a room at the end. The door was open, and the woman explained the layout.

"She had her own hot plate, as you can see, a small bathroom, bed, stereo, TV—everything she wanted."

But Nancy was less interested in the furnishings than in the disarray of clothing left on a chair.

"It looks like she left in a hurry," the girl remarked.

"You think so?" Mrs. Flannery said. "To me, it's just a typical teenager's mess."

Nancy and Ned looked at each other, reserving their answer.

On the desk was a brochure with a photograph of someone attached. Nancy stepped toward it, but Mrs. Flannery sidled in front of it.

"Are you done?" she asked, slipping her hands along the edge of the blotter.

"I'd like to see that pamphlet." Nancy said.

"Pamphlet? What pamphlet?"

"The one you're trying to hide, Mrs. Flannery," Ned replied.

"I'm not doing any such thing," she sputtered, permitting Nancy to pick up the pamphlet. "I just don't think it's right for you to come snooping in here."

Nancy, in the meantime, was studying the cover, which was entitled, *The Most Important Discovery Of Your Life!*

Clipped to it was the picture of an aging man in a long, printed tunic. His stringy, gray hair hung sparsely around his wrinkled face. He was painfully thin, perhaps from frequent fasting, and as she read a few short passages inside the booklet, she realized her assumption was correct.

The man was the ascetic whom Phyllis had chosen to follow. He was Ramaswami!

15

Surprise Return

As Nancy gazed at the small photograph, she spoke to Mrs. Flannery. "This must be the retreat that Phyllis went to," she said, catching the woman's eyes on hers.

"I suppose so."

"Do you know how to get there?" Ned asked, hoping she might reveal an easier access than the one they had taken.

"No. I have no interest in the place whatsoever. Never did and never will."

Nancy, meanwhile, had noticed that there was no specific address given, only a telephone number which she memorized promptly. Aside from that information, there was little else to glean from the pamphlet, so she put it back on the desk.

"Hmm. What's this?" Nancy murmured, spying the edge of a letter that Phyllis had begun to write.

"Now that's really prying," Mrs. Flannery said accusingly, as the girl's fingers slid the paper out from under another one.

To the girl's surprise, there was only the greeting to Angela and a half-finished sentence that read, *I have learned something terr—*.

Terrible or terrific? Nancy wondered. And why had Phyllis left the letter unwritten? Had something urgent interrupted her?

She did not voice her thoughts openly until she and Ned were in the car again. Then, the couple discovered they had reached the same conclusion.

"It's my turn for hunches," Ned said, "and I think Mrs. Flannery knows more than she's telling."

"You get an A-plus." Nancy grinned. "And I'd like to find out what it is."

"Well, maybe if we come back in the dead of night and stalk her every move, we'll be able to—just like that!" Ned snapped his fingers with confidence.

"Not a bad idea," Nancy said. "Not bad at all."

"I was only kidding," her friend replied.

"I know, but I'm not. Maybe we'll bump into Mr. Flannery again!"

"In that case, maybe we ought to bring a policeman along," Ned said.

"With me to protect you?" Nancy teased, raising the boy's eyebrows.

He swung the car onto the street, heading for their next destination, Oberon College. They passed through the busy shopping district into a residential area filled with stately houses. Beyond them was a brown brick wall that surrounded the campus.

"It's pretty, isn't it," Nancy said.

"Not as pretty as Emerson," Ned replied.

Nancy ignored the touch of sour grapes she detected in her friend's voice. "I wonder where the professors' offices are," she went on, still admiring the roll of green lawn that framed the assortment of buildings.

"Over there," Ned said. He indicated a small sign with an arrow that was posted near the parking lot.

They left the car and immediately crossed to

the building that looked more like a small, Tudor mansion than an office.

"Did you call ahead for an appointment?" Ned asked, suddenly realizing that Nancy had not mentioned any specific time they were to see Dr. DeNiro.

"No, I didn't have a chance to, but I'm hoping we'll catch him between classes."

As it was, there seemed to be a steady flow of students on the connecting pathways, and Nancy and Ned gathered momentum. They quickly discovered the professor's door and knocked.

"Come in," a voice replied.

There was a shuffle of papers as the young couple stepped inside.

"Dr. DeNiro, I'm Nancy Drew."

"And I'm Ned Nickerson," Ned said. He stuck out his hand to shake the professor's, but his was hurriedly stuffing a folder into a briefcase.

"I have a class now," the man said briskly.

"Well, we're friends of Bess Marvin and George Fayne. I believe you met them the other day," Nancy said.

"Oh yes, of course."

Suddenly, he let the briefcase tumble on the desk and sat down, gesturing to Nancy and Ned to do the same.

"As a matter of fact, I was planning to call them today," he said.

"You were?" Nancy replied in surprise.

"A most peculiar thing happened yesterday. Here, I'll show you."

He pulled out a lower drawer in his desk and dug to the back for a small packing box. Remaining shreds of brown paper were still wrapped around it. He removed it completely now and opened the lid. Inside was a thick wad of cotton which he drew out quickly.

"Oh!" Nancy exclaimed as a piece of gold jewelry rolled across his palm. "That's Cliff's ring!"

"Are you sure?" Ned asked, taking it from the man and handing it to Nancy.

"It's unmistakably the same one," she replied. "The lily design and the scratches inside. Can you tell me how and where you got this, Dr. DeNiro?"

"It came in the mail," he said. "It was addressed to me here at the college."

"May I see the wrapping paper?" Nancy requested. But to her chagrin, there was no return address on it.

Now she wondered why the ring had been sent to the professor. It seemed to her that his impostor was too clever to have let it slip through his fingers so easily. Might he have given it to someone who forwarded it to Oberon College by mistake?

"Has anything else unusual happened to you recently?" Nancy inquired.

"No, not really. I am busily trying to finish a project—"

"A government project?" Nancy put in, remembering what Bess and George had told her.

"Yes, and I've had my nose buried in books for days."

"I don't mean to pry, Dr. DeNiro," Nancy went on, "but I wonder if the man who was posing as you could be related to your current work."

"Let's say it's not impossible, but unlikely. The same thought occurred to me when I spoke with your friends, but after digesting it a bit, I concluded that my statistical studies would be of little interest to anyone other than someone in my field.

"On the other hand," the instructor continued, "the person could have read my name in the *Gazette* article and conveniently remembered it."

Nancy agreed. "In any case," she said, "I am greatly relieved to have the ring back. Now if we can only find its owner."

Dr. DeNiro's bewildered reaction prompted the girl to explain further. "Sounds like Cliff's in a lot of trouble," the man said, "and if anything relevant should turn up, I will contact you immediately."

"Or, if you can't reach Nancy," Ned inserted, "you can always call me."

They gave him their telephone numbers, which he pocketed, then said he was running late for class. The couple thanked him for his time and followed him up the walkway, separating at the juncture to the parking lot.

"Weird, weird, weird," Ned muttered as he drove the car along the winding pavement.

"And lucky," Nancy said, flashing the ring in her hand.

Suddenly, her eyes settled on a young man carrying a canvas bag toward a campus laundry room. He had brown hair that trailed across his shoulder, and his build was slight like that of the boy she had chased out of the River Heights Theater!

"Slow down, Ned," Nancy said.

The window was down on her side and she stuck her head through it, trying to see the boy's profile as he strode toward a door.

"Who is it?" Ned questioned.

"It looks like the kid I found with Vince in the sound booth," Nancy said.

She opened the car door and stepped out quickly, leaving Ned to idle the engine in a no-parking zone. She raced to the door she had seen the young man go into, but when she looked behind it, he was nowhere in sight.

"Where did he—" Nancy said, in the same instant realizing that he had disappeared around the corner of the building and was running toward a car near a dormitory.

Nancy raced back to Ned's and leaped in.

"We have to follow him," she said. "I'm pretty sure it's the same guy."

The other vehicle now swerved onto the pavement, screeching its wheels as it flew past the couple.

"Did he see you?" Ned said, bearing down on the accelerator.

"I hope not," Nancy said. "I don't think so."

The boy ahead of them cruised down the road in the direction of the business district. He whipped through an amber light just before it turned red, which forced Nancy and Ned to a frustrating halt.

They didn't speak as they watched the silver hatchback dart between cars and pitch through a second light as their own turned green again.

"We can't lose him," Nancy finally said, causing Ned to press down on the pedal.

"Don't worry. We'll catch him," Ned assured her.

The hatchback was still in view, but when a sign for the River Heights Music Festival appeared overhead, the car spun quickly off its track. Ned had been concentrating on it so intently that he did not see another one barreling toward the approaching intersection.

"Watch it, Ned!" Nancy screamed as her eyes caught sight of the sports wagon. But Ned had already sailed into the path of collision!

16

Hazy Report

Instead of jamming on the brakes, which would have been Nancy's instinct, Ned lurched the car forward. The sports wagon careened past the rear bumper, barely missing it before coming to an abrupt halt.

"Why don't you watch where you're going?" the driver yelled back at Ned, then sped around the corner.

Nancy, meanwhile, had sunk against the car seat, feeling the tension in her muscles spin out in a shiver.

"Oh, Ned," she gasped, as he urged the pedal again. "I thought we were going to get crumpled for sure."

"Oh, ye of little faith," Ned said, squeezing her hand lightly. "Now, don't tell me you think I'd foul up a chase by getting us into a car accident."

Nancy shook her head, smiling. "Where did that hatchback go, anyway?" she asked.

"He was heading for the River Heights Theater, and I figure we ought to as well."

"But definitely," Nancy said, straightening up in the seat.

It was amazing how the incident at the intersection, despite the fact that their own car had never stopped moving, had given the hatchback enough time to vanish completely.

"Maybe he turned off onto one of these side streets," Nancy declared. She gazed down the ones they passed, looking for some evidence of the silver car. "I don't see it anywhere," she said at last.

But when they reached the theater, they noticed a trail of engine oil in the driveway and followed it.

"There!" Nancy exclaimed, spotting the elusive hatchback.

It was sitting in a parking space near the manager's office. Ned pulled in next to it and as he shut off the ignition, Nancy stepped out. Ned walked close behind her as she dashed to the door, opening it quickly and announcing herself to an officious-looking secretary.

"Mr. Hillyer is in conference at the moment," was her reply.

Was he talking with the boy whom Nancy suspected had attacked Vince? She and Ned waited a few minutes before interrupting the woman again.

"It's really urgent," Nancy said, half surmising that the manager had given instructions not to admit Nancy.

"As I told you, Mr. Hillyer is tied up. I have no idea how long he will be, and I suggest you call for an appointment."

Nancy strode quickly past the woman, knocking on the office door. She heard two voices clouded by the partition and stepped back, somewhat embarrassed.

The receptionist was on her feet by now and glaring at Nancy. "I suggest you leave," she snapped.

"We can't," Ned returned with equal briskness.

The woman gritted her teeth and pressed the

intercom, advising the manager, "Miss Drew is here and she refuses to go."

"I'll be right out."

As the man emerged in the doorway, Nancy observed someone in the visitor's chair. His hair peeked out from the high back.

"Shall I have you thrown out of here by our security guards?" Mr. Hillyer rasped.

Nancy overlooked the comment. "I have reason to believe that the young man in your office clubbed Vince over the head last night."

"That is absolutely preposterous," the manager said.

"But I told you before how a boy almost knocked me down as he came out of the sound booth only minutes before I found Vince."

Hillyer had intentionally closed his ears. "He happens to be the son of a fine family from Castleton. He called me this morning about a job. He's had some experience in summer theater and we may hire him, especially since he just completed course work at Oberon with honors.

"Frankly, Miss Drew, knowing that we don't have your wholehearted support on the subject, I probably *will* hire him."

"But—" Nancy said, still trying to capture the man's attention.

"Good-bye, Miss Drew, and please don't bother me again."

Nancy knew it was useless to inquire about the boy's name, because neither Hillyer nor his receptionist would volunteer it. Nonetheless, she had picked up some interesting tidbits which she stored for future reference.

"Come on, Ned," she said, pausing to look at the performance schedule on an outside bulletin board.

The word POSTPONED had been stamped across two programs, including a spectacular trio of violinists and what had been advertised as the rare appearance of a famous jazz pianist. The Jansen production, however, seemed to be continuing.

"I'm game for another round of *Oklahoma*," Ned smiled. "Maybe we can at least see two scenes worth—"

"Before the stage collapses?" Nancy laughed. "Well, I had something else in mind for this evening—like a trip to the old Flannery homestead!"

"I knew you wouldn't give up on that one,"

Ned sighed. "In that case, I'd better do a little weight lifting this afternoon to build up these tired muscles."

"And I'm going to put in a call to the swami's retreat," Nancy said.

They returned to the Drew home, where they agreed on a time to meet later.

"See you at nine," Ned said, and drove away.

Nancy hurried into the house, where to her amazement she found Hannah in a complete dither. She had personally called Chief McGinnis to inquire about the ongoing search for Cliff.

"The police think they've found him!"she exclaimed.

"What?" Nancy replied.

Could it be possible that the young man and his intriguing ring had been discovered the same day?

Hannah bobbed her head excitedly. "Yes, it's true. It's true. The chief says someone saw him hitchhiking. The description fits, according to what he told me."

"Where is he now?" Nancy pressed.

"We don't know, exactly," Hannah said, losing some of the animation in her face. "All they

146

have is a report, and they're scouring the area where he was seen."

Nancy now dialed headquarters, asking to be put through to the chief at once. Within seconds, she was told a similar version of the story.

Chief McGinnis chuckled, however. "We get reports like these all the time, you know," he said, "and I'm afraid Hannah has been so worried about Cliff's kidnapping that she didn't hear my final comment before she hung up."

"What was it, Chief?" Nancy inquired.

"Just that eight out of ten reports on missing persons don't usually lead anywhere."

The disappointment Nancy felt was no less than Hannah's when she related her conversation.

"No matter what the chief says," Nancy remarked, "I intend to remain optimistic."

"Good girl," Hannah said, hugging her. "And when that young man comes back, I'm going to bake him the biggest coconut layer cake he ever laid eyes on!"

"Mm, sounds delicious," Nancy said, sniffing the faint odor of something else in the oven.

"Oh! The tarts!" Hannah cried. "They'll burn for sure!"

She dashed into the kitchen, leaving the young detective alone to mull over the numerous details in the mysteries that beset her. Suddenly, she realized that only she and Ned knew about the unexpected return of Cliff's ring, and she raced upstairs to her room. She sprawled out on the bed, resting the telephone alongside her.

She called Bess and George first, then her father. All of them were ecstatic about the discovery.

As it entrenched itself in her mind, Nancy finished her conversation with Mr. Drew and closed her eyes. She saw the gold ring swirl vigorously around the figure of a man whose face was indistinct. But as she ran toward him, a beard grew along the chin, then floated away, leaving a smooth complexion and large eyes several shades darker than his skin.

"Jhaveri," Nancy murmured before slipping into a deeper sleep.

When she awoke, she discovered the phone partly off the hook and a twilight haze creeping between the trees outside her window. She jolted out of bed, resetting the receiver, and changed into slacks and a light sweater.

The dinner hour faded quickly as the young detective let a large noodle slide off her fork.

"Why didn't I think of it before!" she exclaimed.

"What, dear?" Carson Drew inquired.

"The ring!" Nancy said excitedly.

In the course of her nap, two elements of the mystery had joined themselves—Cliff's jewelry and Mr. Jhaveri's jewelry store. Flannery, alias DeNiro, had been there on one occasion, at least. Had he tried to sell the ring to Mr. Jhaveri after stealing it from Bess and George?

"I have an idea that Mr. Jhaveri wanted to ship it back for some reason," Nancy said. "Since the man had introduced himself as Dr. DeNiro from Oberon College, Mr. Jhaveri sent the ring there!"

17

Moonlight Intruder

Nancy's declaration about Cliff's ring caused Mr. Drew to smile. "I assume, then, you are planning a trip back to Mr. Jhaveri's shop," he said.

His daughter grinned. "First, however, I'm going to do a little investigating around the Flannery house. Ned said he'd go with me."

"When is that scheduled for?"

"In about two hours," Nancy said.

"Tonight?" the attorney questioned in surprise.

Nancy related her visit with Mrs. Flannery and her determination to find out whether the man who called himself by the same name was her husband.

"He wasn't there this morning," Nancy said, "but I figure he ought to show up eventually."

Although the young detective would have liked to reveal everything that had occurred during the day, she chose not to. She knew, for instance, that Mr. Hillyer's reaction to her would upset her father unnecessarily, so she avoided the subject.

"I think I'm on the way to convincing the mayor of my innocence," Mr. Drew said unexpectedly.

"That's terrific, Dad," Nancy replied.

It was the first time he had even made reference to the situation in a while. Yet, despite the note of optimism, Nancy did not see an observable change in her father's face. He still seemed distressed.

"So I don't want you to worry anymore," he continued.

Had he only told her half the truth in order to allay her fears? Nancy wondered. But she didn't ask any questions, allowing the rest of the meal to pass quietly.

Before long it was nine o'clock, and Nancy slipped into a jacket, thinking Ned would arrive punctually. To her surprise, though, half an hour had elapsed when the bell finally rang.

"I tried calling you this afternoon, but all I got was a busy signal," Ned said. He explained that his parents had asked him to do a number of errands and he knew he'd be late.

Nancy promptly recalled how the phone receiver had slipped off the hook as she slept next to it.

"I wonder if I missed any other important calls," she said, waving good-bye to her father.

"Well, if you did, I'm sure they'll call back," Ned declared.

The couple strolled across the driveway to Ned's car, unaware for the moment of the silver hatchback that was parked a short distance up the street. In spite of the moonlight that glinted on the hood, it remained concealed under a low-hanging tree. The driver, however, kept his gaze steady on the Drew house.

When Ned finally backed the car out onto the street, the hatchback's headlights turned on and the engine started to purr. The driver waited several seconds before pulling away from the curb, then followed the young detectives.

They headed for the Flannery house. Ned had paid only scant attention to the car in the rearview mirror. It had maintained a fair distance, but when Ned's car halted at the end of a block, the hatchback suspended the chase, waiting for the pair to emerge.

"The downstairs lights are still on," Nancy said to Ned as she gazed at the Flannery house.

"If we see the guy you're looking for," Ned said, "do you want to talk to him?"

"I'm not sure. Let's play it by ear."

"Okay. You're the boss on this one."

"Gee, thanks," Nancy smiled.

Together, they stole up the driveway, hiding behind a tree trunk when Mrs. Flannery moved in front of the living room window.

"Did she see us?" Ned asked.

"I don't think so."

But the girl knew their shadows could be seen on the pavement. She shrunk back, leaning against the bark. From where they stood, they were able to see a back window as well, and as one light in the front turned off, others switched on in the kitchen.

"Somebody's eating," Ned commented. He had craned his neck to peer between the lower branches and caught sight of black hair. "Come on. Let's get closer," the boy said.

They ducked out from their secret place and edged forward, stopping only when they heard the kitchen window being cranked open. Instantly, the two young people dodged discovery, pulling next to the house and accidentally stepping into a garden of petunias.

"Yuck," Ned said as he shook dirt off his sneakers.

Nancy, however, was more concerned about the footprints that might be noticed, and sprang to the ground to cover them up quickly. As she did so, voices drifted outside. One was low, yet recognizable.

"That is the man we saw at Swain Lake Lodge!" she told Ned.

After all the mysteries she had solved, she had learned to use all her senses with amazing accuracy.

"How can you be so positive?" Ned whispered.

"Trust me," the girl said, raising a finger to her lips.

Then, even Ned heard Nancy's name! But what precisely was being said about her?

Nancy closed her eyes to concentrate, but the whistle of a boiling teakettle interfered. She was also oblivious to the figure crouched behind the front hedge. It was the driver of the hatchback. He had crept up the sidewalk when

154

the couple moved up the Flannery's driveway and darted behind bushes before coming to a standstill.

Ned, in the meantime, had let Nancy slip forward under the kitchen window.

"If she comes snooping around here again," the man was saying, "you know what to do."

"Sure, and I'll dump her at the lake."

Nancy winced, imagining another horrifying night in the forest shelter. Or worse, she thought.

"Well, she won't be back," Mrs. Flannery continued. "Good thing you waited until now to come home."

"When she trailed us out to the house on River Lane," her husband said, "I figured she'd turn up here sooner or later."

There was a clatter of cups and saucers and the sound of running water which interrupted the conversation temporarily. Then the lights went out, plunging the driveway into total darkness.

Instantly, the figure behind the hedge bolted toward Ned and seized him from behind, chopping a well-placed blow to the neck. The boy sank to the ground without a cry.

Nancy let out a shriek, quelling it as the boy dived for her too!

Now the lights went on in the kitchen again, and the back door opened and closed.

"Who's out there?" came Flannery's deep voice.

Nancy turned as the boy's fist shoved her down on the pavement, causing her to roll within inches of the man's feet. He grabbed her quickly, and dragged her into the backyard, and up the porch steps, letting her attacker escape.

"Let go of—" she cried, but he covered her mouth with his hand.

"What about her friend in the driveway?" Flannery's wife said.

"Just leave him. We'll be gone from here long before he comes to."

Nancy struggled as the pair secured her to a chair, binding her arms and legs so tightly she felt almost nauseated.

"You can't get away with this," the girl said, causing Mrs. Flannery to stick a soft roll in her mouth.

Nancy bit into it angrily, gulping down part of it. The rest broke off, dribbling crumbs on the floor.

"Was that good?" the woman sneered. "Here, have another piece."

She took a larger chunk of bread this time and stuffed it in Nancy's mouth.

"Where's Singh's car?" the woman now asked her husband.

"Up at the retreat."

As the young detective listened, questions whirled through her brain. What was the men's connection with the retreat? Was Ramaswami involved with them and the retreat merely a cover-up? Or was the swami being used in some evil way?

If only the Flannerys would reveal more information! Nancy thought.

But they disappeared upstairs, leaving her alone for almost twenty minutes. The sound of hurried footsteps creaking across the floor above convinced her they were packing.

Maybe Ned would come to sooner than they expected, Nancy hoped, but that did not prove to be the case.

It was almost two hours later before the young man regained consciousness. A dull ache drove across his spine as he realized he was lying along the edge of the Flannery's driveway. A stray petunia wrapped around the toe of his sneaker reminded him of the sequence of events.

"Nancy?" he muttered weakly, but there was no answer.

He lifted his head slowly, the pain doubling rapidly and forcing him to drop it again.

"Nancy, where are you?" he cried out louder than before.

But the only response was the pad of a cat across the driveway into the yard of an empty house, causing the young man to roll on his side. He looked toward the kitchen window that was closed now. Nancy, who had stood under it, was gone! Surely she would not have left Ned as she had unless someone had overtaken her, too! Who was it—the same stranger who had attacked Ned?

18

Scorpion Scare

Soon after the incident had occurred, the driver of the hatchback had leaped out of sight. He had raced the car down to the corner and swerved onto a main road that led to the River Heights Theater.

The Jansen troupe's performance was under way, and the boy determined there was only an hour left before it finished. He turned into the parking area, which was less full than the night before, and stopped his car near the exit. He jumped out, holding a metal canister with punctures in the lid.

Smirking, he darted into the empty lobby, where he waited a moment as the buoyant melody emanating from the orchestra began to end. He then opened the door a crack, removed the lid of the canister, and freed from its prison a large, black scorpion. Urged forward, the insect crawled out, revealing its monstrous claws and poisonous sting!

The boy pulled back, shutting the door without being seen and listening for the first shriek of discovery.

The venomous animal, however, followed an even trail down the middle of the aisle until it was past the halfway mark. Then the glow of stage lights captured it and several couples in end seats screamed frantically.

"Help!" a woman cried as the jointed legs of the scorpion scurried off the carpet.

The man seated next to her shouted over the growing din in the audience. "It's a scorpion!" he exclaimed.

"Take the side exits!" another voice yelled.

Now the pandemonium struck the performers. The conductor ordered the musicians to leave the pit and the actors on stage fell into disarray as the house lights came up, sending the scorpion under a row of now-vacant seats.

"This is the last straw," one woman snapped in disgust as she charged out of the theater. "I

wouldn't come here again if you paid me!"

Her complaints were echoed by practically everyone who fled through the lobby in fear of the venomous creature.

"Please—please," the festival manager muttered helplessly. "We'll take care of everything."

But his weak promises went unheard, as he watched the departing crowd head for the parking lot. There the boy who had deposited the scorpion in the theater laughed. He waited, however, until the last car left, then went back inside where the festival manager had called the police to report the incident.

The manager was asking for emergency assistance as the boy stepped forward.

"Gee, what happened, Mr. Hillyer?" he asked.

"Oh, Brady," the manager replied. "Somebody let a scorpion loose in the theater."

"That's terrible," the boy said, trying not to appear overly concerned as he went on. "Do you suppose you'll have to shut down the festival after all?"

"I guess your real concern is whether we'll be able to give you the job we talked about."

"Yes, sir," Brady said.

Mr. Hillyer heaved a long, steady sigh. "Frankly, my boy, I doubt that the festival can last much longer. The Jansen troupe has already informed me they are canceling their contract with us."

His listener was almost gleeful to hear the news, but he remained solemn.

"So maybe if the Castleton Theater still wants them," Brady said, "the Jansen company will go back there."

"We've had problems ever since Jansen made the last-minute switch," the manager said.

"As you know, Pa works the sound booth for the Castleton Theater," the boy replied, "and he told me all about it."

Hillyer was too distraught to pursue the conversation further. He let the young man leave when the police arrived. Brady hopped into his car, turned the radio up, and drove away.

Ned, in the meantime, had managed to pull himself off the Flannerys' driveway. He dragged his feet toward the backyard, noting darkness throughout the house. He told himself that he would risk an unpleasant encounter with the couple when he inquired about Nancy.

But as he climbed the porch steps, he noticed a trail of bread crumbs.

That's odd, he thought. Why would anyone throw out food for birds at night?

He didn't think about it further as he knocked on the door. No one came, however. Maybe they couldn't hear him, he surmised, and he darted to the front, still trying to ignore the throb under his skull.

He rang the bell a long time. There was still no answer. Had the Flannerys left the house?

As Ned returned to his car, he did not observe the flat tire against the curb. He started the ignition and began to steer, rolling the vehicle forward. Suddenly, he was aware that one wheel was spinning on its rim. He cut off the engine and jumped out to examine it. The small valve cap on the tire had been removed and air had been allowed to escape!

Had his attacker done this? Ned wondered. Yet, somehow, that idea was hard to comprehend. How, for instance, could the stranger have abducted Nancy and pulled off the nozzle without her slipping away? Perhaps there were two people involved in the abduction.

Before he could mull over the question, Ned dived into his trunk and took out an air pump which he quickly hooked up. He gazed along the curb for the missing cap and discovered it had been thrown up on someone's lawn.

Several minutes later he was on his way to the Drew house, where a downstairs light had been left on for Nancy. It was approaching midnight as the boy pressed the bell.

It was a surprise that Hannah, rather than Mr. Drew, came to the door.

"Is Mr. Drew asleep?" Ned asked as the housekeeper's eyes traveled beyond the boy.

"Where's Nancy?" she said, disregarding his question.

"She's gone."

From the somber tone of the boy's voice, Hannah knew that trouble lurked in his explanation.

"Mr. Drew received an urgent call from the police," she said. "He's been down at the River Heights Theater for almost forty-five minutes."

Ned quickly revealed what had happened to him, adding, "Nancy just vanished into thin air."

"Oh, dear," the woman frowned. "Well, don't waste your time here. You'd better find Mr. Drew right away."

The young man pulled out of the driveway,

165

still feeling sluggish, but he propelled himself as fast as he could to the theater. When he arrived, he was astonished to find the lawyer defending himself against Hillyer's rash accusations.

"*That* is all *your* fault!" the manager grumbled. He was pointing to an empty metal canister and another container alongside it that now held the dead scorpion.

"You are being ridiculous," Mr. Drew said in an even voice. "How could I have any connection with what happened here tonight?"

"Ever since you forced the Jansen troupe out of their arrangement in Castleton—"

"I didn't force them, Mr. Hillyer. The town of River Heights made an offer which received the approval of every board member. I, for one, did not even know that Jansen had a pre-existing deal with Castleton. The mayor of River Heights informed me he had seen them perform elsewhere and suggested we line them up here. When I called their business manager, he made only a glib reference to a pending contract. But the impression he gave me was that it wasn't very satisfactory. It isn't my fault they accepted our proposal instead. Obviously, it was a better one than Castleton's!"

Mr. Drew had spoken with a clarity that rivaled the temper of his listener.

"All I know," Hillyer went on, "is that we will lose a tremendous amount of money if we have to close down the festival."

"Mr. Hillyer, rather than sputtering about that, wouldn't it behoove us all to try and figure out who is causing all the trouble?"

Although Mr. Drew had seen Ned, the intensity of his conversation and the police officers who flanked the two men prevented him from addressing the boy. Ned, also, did not wish to interrupt. But as the discussion wore on, he listened with greater interest.

"Tell me, Mr. Hillyer, did you not see anyone strange enter the premises?" one officer questioned.

The manager had steered his vision away from Mr. Drew. "No, I told you that before."

"But who was that kid with the long hair?"

"He must've been passing by when he saw the mass exodus. He knew the show couldn't have finished yet, so he decided to find out what had happened."

"What's the boy's name?" Mr. Drew inquired, but Hillyer continued to direct his statements to the policeman.

167

"We'd like that information, if you don't mind," the officer countered.

"Brady Tilson."

"And what's your connection with him?"

"I don't have a connection, officer. I merely offered him a job this morning."

Now Ned stepped closer, wondering: Was this the boy whom he and Nancy had followed from Oberon College? If so, he was the one whom Nancy suspected of having attacked Vince, the sound and lighting technician! Had he returned again to plant the poisonous scorpion?

As the men's conversation diverted to the exact moment when the disruption had occurred, Mr. Drew spoke. "From what I overheard Mr. Hillyer say earlier, Brady arrived only minutes after the trouble started—around ten o'clock or so."

"Ten-thirty would be more exact," an officer put in.

Ten-thirty, Ned repeated to himself. That was only a short time after his attack. Might there be a connection between the two events?

19

Prisoners' Retreat

Ned let the men finish speaking before he took Mr. Drew aside. The festival manager glanced gruffly at the boy as the officers made a few final statements.

"What's up, Ned?" Mr. Drew said, adding, "I assume that you dropped Nancy off at the house."

"No, sir. I-I don't know where she is."

The lawyer could see a visible tremble in the boy's body. "Tell me everything that happened, and don't leave anything out," he said.

But before the young collegian could complete his story, the festival manager and the police began to leave the building.

"Everybody out, Mr. Drew," Mr. Hillyer said

sharply, leading the way to an exit.

"We'll talk again tomorrow," the attorney informed the man.

"Not if I can help it," he said.

"Well, I'm afraid you may not have a choice in the matter," one of the officers said from behind.

When they were all outside, Mr. Drew requested the policeman join him and Ned.

"I couldn't help overhearing the discussion about Brady Tilson," Ned told the young officer.

"Do you know him?"

"No."

"But my daughter Nancy apparently had an encounter with him last night," Mr. Drew put in.

"That's right," Ned continued. He explained the sequence of events in the sound booth just as Nancy had related them to him. "But when we came to see Mr. Hillyer this morning, he ignored us."

"As you can see, officer," the attorney went on, "Mr. Hillyer refuses to listen to anything from the lips of anyone named Drew."

The policeman nodded. He would have called Hillyer back from the parking lot, but following Mr. Drew's remark, realized he would just be inviting another unproductive scene.

"When can we talk to your daughter?" the officer inquired.

"That's another problem," Ned answered for Mr. Drew. He displayed the welt across his neck and told how he had been struck from behind.

"Nancy's been hard at work on the kidnapping of that young amnesia patient," Mr. Drew said, assuming the disappearance was well-known in the River Heights police department. "Tonight she and Ned went on a small excursion to the home of Mr. and Mrs. Flannery."

The officer seemed puzzled. "What's their connection?" he asked.

"Well, I think Nancy suspected Mr. Flannery of being the person who attacked Cliff in the hospital," Mr. Drew said. "She wasn't absolutely positive, however. Did you run into the man?" he asked Ned.

"Yes and no. We overheard him mention Nancy's name, but we didn't see the face, so I'm not a hundred percent sure he's the one we saw at the lodge."

"Any idea who gave you the welt?" the policeman questioned.

"That's what I've been leading up to. I have a hunch it could be Brady Tilson," Ned answered.

"And not Flannery," Mr. Drew interposed.

"No, definitely not. He and his wife were still inside when I was hit."

The young man blinked his eyes wearily, and he swayed off one foot as the adventures of the evening swirled through his head.

"We'll search the Flannery place now," the officer assured Mr. Drew. "Maybe your daughter's still there."

Although Ned was positive Nancy had been taken away by someone, he knew he had no evidence to prove it. No one had come to the door when he knocked and rang, but that didn't mean the young detective wasn't trapped inside.

"Can I go with you?" the boy asked the officer. He shook his head.

"Do me a favor, son. Go home and get a good night's rest—unless you want to have that bruise checked first. You could have a slight concussion, you know."

Ned insisted he felt fine, but Mr. Drew studied his weary face. "You'll stay in the guest room tonight," he said. "I'll call your family and explain. I'm sure it'll be all right."

The young man nodded gratefully.

"What about Nancy, though?" he asked.

"I'm afraid we'll have to leave everything up to the police now," Mr. Drew sighed.

He himself was deeply worried about his daughter's safety, but he managed to retain his composure after the police said they would contact him shortly.

By next morning, however, the telephone had not rung and the attorney dialed headquarters. He learned that the Flannery house was vacant. Teacups and saucers that had been left in the sink overnight indicated that the occupants had departed recently. Officers, nevertheless, intended to search the grounds in daylight.

When Ned finally awoke, Mr. Drew relayed the information, asking if any other clues to Nancy's whereabouts had occurred to the boy.

"Just that I'm positive she's with the Flannerys," he said. "At first, I thought the guy who hit me had probably kidnapped Nancy. But if Brady was my attacker, then he obviously didn't take Nancy with him to the theater."

"Well, I think the police must've come to the same conclusions by now," Mr. Drew said. "So where do you suppose Flannery is?"

"Maybe at Swain Lake Lodge."

Mr. Drew considered the idea. "I doubt it. He wouldn't want to be seen in a public place with his prisoner."

"Then, maybe—" Ned let the sentence hang, thinking momentarily about Phyllis Pruett.

He shot out of his chair to the telephone. He didn't know Angela's number, but he quickly obtained it from the River Heights Theater office and dialed again.

"Angela Pruett?" the young man said, "This is Ned Nickerson."

From there on in, plans were made for him to pick her up at her hotel. He gave only a brief explanation before turning to Mr. Drew again.

"I'm going to find the swami's retreat if it's the last thing I do," he announced, "because that's where I think Nancy is!"

"Perhaps you ought to take along some extra muscle," the attorney said, "like Bess and George and the boys."

"Excellent idea," Ned declared. "Would you like to come too, sir?"

"Seems to me you have a full car already," Mr. Drew said, "but I wouldn't miss this trip for anything. I'll follow in my car."

It took almost an hour before Ned was able to round up everyone. Bess and George were completely shocked by the news of Nancy's abduction. Angela was equally astounded by the connection unraveling between the Flannerys and her own sister's disappearance.

"And what about Cliff?" Bess said.

The detectives wondered if they were on the right track. Had the retreat really become a hideaway for prisoners?

Mr. Drew followed the group in his own car, having left a strict message with Hannah not to reveal their destination to anyone. He did, however, pass the word along to Chief McGinnis.

The most pressing concern at the moment, though, was how to reach the retreat. Since their harrowing experience on the trail, Nancy and Ned had not returned to hunt for a road.

"Even so," Ned told his friends, "somebody near the lake must know if one exists. If not, we'll have to traipse through the woods."

"Uh-oh," Bess said, glancing at her bare ankles. "Hope we don't get bitten along the way."

"You should've thought of that sooner," her cousin said.

"Well, I can't think of everything, George Fayne."

Dave interrupted unexpectedly. "It seems to me that you two enjoy picking on each other," he said.

"We're not picking on each other," Bess said defensively. "George is merely looking out for my best interest."

Her friend pursed his lips, swallowing his words, as George giggled. Burt, meanwhile, had asked to look at the road map Ned kept in the glove compartment.

"Swain Lake isn't far from the airport," Ned told him, which helped the Emerson boy locate it more quickly.

"As I recall," Burt remarked, "there's a road that runs up into the hill around that area."

"You're probably thinking of the one Nancy and I were on the other day," Ned said. "It leads to the lodge, but not to the retreat, which I assume is somewhere at the foot of the lake."

"Come to think of it," George said to Bess, "don't you remember Nancy saying that Cliff was found near the airport?"

"Yes, that's right," Bess said excitedly. "It's possible that he was on his way back from the retreat!"

"Or on the way to it," George said. "At the moment, it really doesn't matter which direction he was heading—just that he was in the vicinity."

"I vote we go to the airport," Bess told Ned.

"I agree," Angela said.

"Maybe we will find an access to the retreat, after all," Dave encouraged their driver.

"You could be right," Ned replied, and when signs for the airport came within view, he followed them.

The airport itself had been modernized during the past year. New terminals had sprung up, and according to all reports, another one would be under construction shortly. Mr. Drew was temporarily bewildered as he kept his car in line with Ned's, wondering why they had veered off in this direction. Nonetheless, when the young man waved in the rearview mirror, the lawyer knew there was a reason.

It did not reveal itself, though, until the travelers climbed a steep road that curved away from the airport and into a densely wooded area. The road sloped toward a gully, weaving a thread of narrow pavement around it that unraveled along a large fork of water.

"Look! This has to be Swain Lake!"

George exclaimed to her companions.

She let her eyes trail out over the deep blue pocket, catching sight of a tan car parked by a large cabin. If it hadn't been for the car, she might have missed the building because of its dark log frame that blended against the trees. As Ned drove closer, the girl detective thought she spied a blue racing stripe on the trunk!

"Isn't that Dev Singh's car?" George asked her cousin.

Although neither of them had ever seen it before, it fitted Nancy's description.

"I'm beginning to get jealous," Ned said in a joking tone.

"Of what?" George inquired.

"Well, you both seem more tuned in to every little detail about this case than I am."

"Not every detail," Bess said. "After all, who got to investigate the lodge?"

"And visit Mrs. Flannery," her cousin added.

Ned grinned. "I have a headache to prove it, too!"

He slowed the car, motioning Mr. Drew to look in the direction of the lakeside cabin.

"We're sure that's the swami's retreat!" Ned exclaimed. "Stick close, okay?"

20

Intriguing Discovery

Mr. Drew followed the line of Ned's pointing finger and settled his eyes on the cabin. It stood at the foot of a small, sandy incline several feet from the water, and the attorney concluded that theirs was a back view of the building.

As Ned drove farther, he, too, realized that the cabin was nestled beneath an embankment, carefully concealed by a thickness of trees. Ned almost passed it, but the sound of a sputtering car engine below made him stop.

Was it the tan car George had spotted? the young detectives wondered.

Their driver pulled ahead instantly, burying the car behind a roadside shelter. Mr. Drew

179

followed suit and waited with the young people as the distant engine continued to churn and then stop abruptly.

Ned took the lead now with Nancy's father and crossed the road. They walked behind the trees, keeping the uncovered cabin windows in view at all times. They did not notice any movement until they heard a crackle of twigs and leaves under the steep embankment. Then the group froze.

Had the person who tried to start the tan car seen them?

Bravely, Ned went forward, and the crackling noise stopped. He gulped nervously, wondering if someone would suddenly spring at him, but the silence lasted, and he waved the rest of his friends forward.

"I can't slide down that," Bess whispered to George. She gaped fearfully at the deep spur of slippery gravel beneath them.

"Well, we'll just leave you here, then."

Bess gazed at the forsaken wilderness around her. "I'll go. I'll go," she said, and took Dave's hand.

One by one the group, including Angela, who had remained quiet, strung out along the slope, ducking low as large, almond eyes peered out

of the cabin window. The face pulled back
quickly and the door opened, causing the visitors to drop behind a thick overturned log that
lay near the base of the building.

George's blood pounded through her veins
as she raised her eyes, catching sight of the
stranger as he turned in their direction. It was
Mr. Jhaveri!

Had the River Heights jeweler suddenly become a devotee of the swami? George wondered.

She lowered her head quickly, and they
waited, breathless, for the man to go inside
again. When he finally did, though, he didn't
shut the door fully.

Ned scurried to the back of the building,
taking Burt with him, while the others remained out of sight. The boys discovered a
basement window partially covered by tall
weeds. Tearing them aside, they stared in at
several unmade cots that sagged over the cold,
damp floor.

"Doesn't appeal to me a bit," Burt remarked.
He followed Ned to the far corner, where
another small window revealed the top of
someone's head resting against the wall!

Ned pressed his face against the glass, hoping

to see who it was, but the hair color eluded him in the glare of sunlight. Burt tugged on his arm for some sort of answer, but Ned merely shook his head.

"Nancy? Phyllis?" he called through the crack in the frame. There was no response.

The others, including Mr. Drew, were about to circle in the direction of the parked car when a voice stopped them in their tracks.

"Now, ladies and gentlemen," the man said, flashing a mouthful of gleaming teeth, as the group swung to face him.

"Prem Nath!" Bess exclaimed.

"Ah, so we meet again," he said pleasantly.

He moved out from his hiding place under the embankment and shook the dry earth off his sweater.

"We heard you coming." He grinned.

"We're looking for our friend, Nancy Drew," George said. "This is her father."

"Oh, I'm honored to meet you, sir."

Mr. Drew nodded stiffly. "Where are you keeping her?" he asked.

"Obviously, there is some misunderstanding, Mr. Drew. Your daughter is not here." He paused. "We are peaceful people," he said, but a shout from above broke the calmness in his voice.

"The police are coming!" someone cried. "I just picked it up on the shortwave radio!"

"Let's get out of here!" another voice yelled, pulling Nath out of his tranquil posture.

He dived toward the visitors, pushing his way to the front stairs, but Mr. Drew tackled him.

"Where's my daughter?" he repeated again. His face flushed in anger.

"Let go of me!" the Indian rasped.

Mr. Drew shoved the man back against Bess and George, while Burt and Ned raced to the front, charging into the men who sought to flee the cabin.

"Oh!" Bess shrieked as Dave tripped one of them, causing him to flip over on his back.

Ned recognized him instantly as Keshav Lal, the fellow who had steered him and Nancy down the tortuous trail!

"You creep!" Ned yelled, now aiming for Flannery, who ran down the steps.

Flannery pushed a fist at the boy's jaw, but missed as Ned ducked, grabbing his arm and twisting him to the ground!

Mrs. Flannery, in the meantime, was screaming inside the cabin as Nancy suddenly caught her by surprise. She flung a tablecloth around the woman's waist and dragged her back, throwing her onto the couch.

"Nancy!" George and Bess exclaimed when they saw the titian hair.

They dived past the scuffle on the ground and raced up the steps toward the girl's prisoner, wrapping the cloth in knots around the arm of the sofa.

"Phyllis Pruett and Cliff are here, too!" Nancy told her friends.

"Speaking of Phyllis, where's Angela?" George said suddenly.

"Angela came with you?"

By now, sirens were approaching the cabin, and within seconds, patrol cars had pulled into view. Officers with handguns poised slid down the embankment, capturing the men who had already been subdued by the Emerson boys and Mr. Drew.

"Hands up," a policeman shouted, as the trio slowly got to their feet.

Having heard Nancy's voice, Mr. Drew hurried into the cabin.

"Nancy—you're all right!" he said.

"Oh, Dad, I told you I could take care of myself." Nancy smiled, feeling her eyes grow moist.

Now Ned and the others surrounded her.

"You were all so brave," Nancy told them.

"It was Ned's idea," Bess said, causing the young man to blush.

He slipped his arm around Nancy's shoulder, saying, "I thought you had vanished forever."

"Me? Never," she replied, pecking his cheek and gulping as she remembered the other two captives.

They were already coming up the basement stairs with Mr. Jhaveri behind them. "I freed them, too, Nancy," he said, as Phyllis and Cliff stood in the room.

"Cliff!" Bess exclaimed.

"Correction, please." He grinned. "It's Randy."

"You mean you've got your memory back?" George said gleefully.

"One hundred percent. The minute I saw this place I remembered everything," he said.

Mr. Drew urged everyone to join the police, who had snapped handcuffs on the three men;

and before the former amnesia patient could tell his story, the lawyer hurried toward the underhang where Angela Pruett had secreted herself during the capture.

"We found Phyllis," Mr. Drew said in a quiet voice.

Upon seeing her sister, Angela ran forward and slipped her arms around the girl. "You should never have run away," Angela told her.

"I know, Angie. I'm sorry."

They whispered to each other as Nancy informed the police that Mr. Jhaveri had released her and the other two prisoners.

"Apparently," Nancy said, "he was an innocent victim of his cousin's greed. Keshav Lal had been a disciple of the swami. He was his assistant, as a matter of fact, until recently, when Ramaswami departed for another section of the country. He discovered that Lal had been intercepting valuable gifts to him and selling them through his relative, Mr. Jhaveri.

"Mr. Flannery here even tried to sell a beautiful gold ring which belonged to Randy. That was Flannery's big mistake."

Nancy's friends stepped closer.

"You see," Nancy went on, "we had told Mr.

Jhaveri about the ring on different occasions. He had seen Bess and George hand it over to Flannery, who at the time called himself Dr. DeNiro, and when he was asked to sell it, Mr. Jhaveri panicked."

"I know I should have immediately returned it to the girls," the jeweler said, "but I was frightened, really scared. If I told them how it had come into my possession, I would have had to tell them about Keshav. He had often given me trinkets to sell for him. I never questioned him about them, and he never discussed where they came from. But when he brought in the ring, I realized his friend had stolen it from the girls. So far as I knew, he was Dr. DeNiro from Oberon College, and I shipped it back to him, hoping he wouldn't bother me again."

Now Randy spoke. "I had come to the retreat frequently. It was almost like home to me, I suppose, because of my childhood days in India. My parents are still serving as missionaries there, and before I left for the states to study, they gave me a maharajah's ring. He presented it to them in exchange for all they had done for his people. I, in turn, had been thinking of giving it to Ramaswami to help him with his work.

"But the last weekend I spent here, I remember feeling very uneasy. I had spoken to Lal about the ring, and I would have given it to him for the swami, except that I overheard Lal's conversation with Dev Singh."

Randy now glanced at Prem Nath. "This man here," he said. "Believe me, Mr. Singh, I will make sure that Ramaswami gets *his* ring!"

So Randy's kidnapper had cleverly falsified an immigration card to cover up his real identity! How shrewd he had been to have it ready when the young detectives and the police challenged him on River Lane!

"Anyway," Randy went on, "I realized Lal had started a little business for himself at the swami's expense. So I waited for a chance to see Ramaswami alone, and when I did, I told him everything, not realizing that Lal was listening. I left quickly then. I didn't have a car, so I hitchhiked some distance and cut through the woods toward the airport. Next thing I knew, Lal and Singh had jumped me. They apparently didn't have time to hunt for the ring in my knapsack."

"They left it up to Flannery to retrieve it," Nancy remarked.

As she spoke, the captives fixed their jaws angrily and Phyllis offered her story. She said she had run away from home. "I was just mixed up at the time," she stated. "Angie, you have to believe me. I wasn't trying to hurt anyone."

"I believe you, Phyllis," Angela Pruett answered gently, urging her sister to continue.

"I was so upset," Phyllis said, "that when I heard about the swami's retreat, I thought to myself, that's for me—peace and quiet. It was great, too, until I overheard the Flannerys talking about Ramaswami. They said Keshav was worried he would find out what they were all up to.

"So I assume Mr. Lal wrote those messages that were supposedly from you just to make me think you were all right," Angela interjected. She looked at the prisoner whose face had settled into a rigid stare.

"I was determined to warn the swami. Of course, I didn't know that Randy had already done so," Phyllis went on. "But before I could pack or write you a note, Angie, the Flannerys pulled me out of my room and forced me into their car. Mr. Flannery drove me up here and threw me into the cellar, where he tied me up."

189

The conversation now shifted to the attack on Ned. "I saw the boy who did it," Nancy admitted. "He's the one who knocked out Vince."

"Well, if you can make a positive identification," her father replied, "then that little case will be solved too."

"One question still," George interrupted. "Who called the police today?"

"Your housekeeper, Mr. Drew," one of the officers said. "Chief McGinnis said you had told him where you were headed, but it was Mrs. Gruen who pressed us into action."

"Thank goodness for Hannah," grinned Nancy, as the prisoners were led away.

While the disappearances of Randy and Phyllis had been solved, it was only during the next couple of days that the problems surrounding the River Heights Theater began to straighten out.

Brady Tilson was brought in for questioning and he reluctantly admitted his guilt. He had created all the disruption at the theater because he wanted to force a shutdown. He said his father had lost his job at Castleton's outdoor pavilion because Castleton had been unable to replace the Jansen troupe on such short notice.

River Heights, Brady claimed, had actually stolen Castleton's production and audience, and he was determined to get it back! The first thing he did was to steal the festival's mailing list and pick up handfuls of fliers left on a table in the River Heights Theater lobby. He then stamped CANCELLED on them, and sent them out to as many people as possible.

When Mr. Hillyer heard the story, he sent a personal apology to Mr. Drew and Nancy, noting that Vince, the sound technician, had verified everything. At the same time, telephone calls from the mayor and various board members besieged the Drew household, causing Nancy to wonder if the flood of apologies and compliments would ever end.

Despite the excitement, however, she could not help thinking of where her next adventure would lead. To her amazement, she would soon find herself on the trail of *The Kachina Doll Mystery!*

In the meantime, she would enjoy the feast which Hannah had been preparing for days. When Randy arrived with Phyllis and Angela, they peeked into the kitchen, but the housekeeper had scooted them out quickly.

She reappeared only when Bess, George, and the Emerson boys arrived. Nancy had counted the plates and discovered two extras. But before she could say anything, Hannah told everyone to close their eyes.

"We have two surprise guests this evening!"

"Hi, Nancy!" a small voice giggled, causing all eyes to open. It was Tommy Johnson, and with him was Lisa Scotti!

The little boy was still wearing a leg cast, but with Lisa's help, he hobbled quickly toward the young detective and hugged her.

"Oh, Tommy, you look wonderful!" Nancy cried happily.

Knowing that the men responsible for Tommy's injuries would now face a stiff penalty was enough to satisfy the onlookers—Nancy, in particular.

She grinned at Hannah. "I'd like to give special thanks to the person who really saved the day for all of us!" Nancy exclaimed.

Everyone applauded enthusiastically, but following Hannah's signal of modesty, turned their applause toward Nancy.

"You really deserve it," Ned whispered to the young detective.